Part the FIRST

In which King Henry II of England kicks an officious envoy of the pope down a flight of steps, and Princess Alys tells the King's mistress why she hates her fiancé, Prince Richard.

Windsor Castle to the West of London, by a day's horse ride - 20th, August 1171

Queen Eleanor of England and Aquitaine gripped the arms of her seat in fear for her safety, waiting for the coming onslaught. Although she was seated on the periphery of the dais, she knew from painful experience that when her husband's temper was roused, anybody within range of his fists or feet or sword could suffer imminent death.

Accustomed to his explosive temper, and known to give as good as she received, even the Queen was shocked by his sudden violent outburst against the cardinal. The fat pompous cleric, looking more like a throbbing red pustule about to erupt than a Prince of the Church, was acting as though he, rather than King Henry, had been anointed by God as ruler of the nation.

The ridiculous narcissistic little man stood and pontificated before the front of the throne, preaching with imperial authority, invoking the judgement of God and Jesus, pointing his finger at the King's chest, denouncing him and threatening the monarch of all England and half of France with the wrath of all the angels in heaven.

Yet to the Cardinal's surprise, as well as that of the entire court, everything changed in an instant. One moment, the Cardinal was standing on his feet, held fast by the authority of the Catholic Church; the next moment, the silly cleric was flying backwards through the air like a fat fish leaping rearward out of a stream.

Without any warning, King Henry screamed an abuse and planted his boot in the man's belly. With the strength of a bucking stallion, Henry kicked the Cardinal off the dais. The Papal Legate launched into the air like a rock from a ballista, flew in silent amazement through the air, and landed on his back with a sickening thud three steps below the throne.

ALAN GOLD

THE BOOK OF ALYS

HENRY II, exhausted from everlasting war, finds solace, passion, and tragedy falling for the youthful beauty of ALYS

First published by Romaunce Books in 2023
Suite 2, Top Floor, 7 Dyer Street, Cirencester, Gloucestershire, GL7 2PF

© Alan Gold, Sydney Australia, November 2022

Alan Gold has asserted his right under the Copyright Designs and Patents
Act 1988 to be identified as the author of this work.

A catalogue record for this book is available from the British Library

The Book of Alys
Paperback ISBN 978-1-73918-570-1

Cover design and content by Ray Lipscombe

Printed and bound in Great Britain
Romaunce Books™ is a registered trademark

ALAN GOLD
THE BOOK
OF ALYS

HENRY II, exhausted from everlasting war, finds solace,
passion, and tragedy falling for the youthful beauty of ALYS

Contents

Only then did the Cardinal utter a shriek of fear. The King sprang up from his throne and stormed down to where the shocked cleric had just landed, and with each step, screamed an ungodly series of filthy curses at him invoking all the devils in Hell.

King Henry's wild eyes and puce face presaged the death of the Papal Legate at any moment, or failing that, the death of anybody within the range of the King's fists. The entire court stood stock still, too shocked and terrified to move. When the tall and muscular monarch paced from his throne and thundered down the three steps of the dais, drawing his sword and thrusting it at the neck of the terrified priest, the entire court knew that anybody who spoke or even moved could be next to meet their maker.

Eleanor looked on in concern. If Henry killed the Pope's emissary, as he was certainly about to, then it would mean war between France and England. And from the look on the King's face, the hapless priest lying on the ground, arms and legs flailing like a gigantic red cockroach, was within moments of being butchered, breathing his last, sliced open like a pig from neck to gizzard. Eleanor was tempted to jump up and restrain her husband, but after all these years, she knew that she'd be the one against whom he'd turn in his uncontrollable fury. So she forced herself to remain seated and allow fate to determine whether or not death would soon visit this Cardinal, a diminutive self-righteous minion whom Pope Alexander III had sent from the Vatican, a little functionary who'd dared to stand before King Henry and order him to obey the Holy See's command.

Queen Eleanor considered herself lucky that on this occasion, the king's vicious temper was aimed not at her or their children, but at the wretched priest who remained sprawled on the floor in front of the throne's dais, staring up in wide-eyed horror at his nemesis. The Cardinal's once florid and offensively confident face had suddenly blanched white with shock, pain and horror.

As Eleanor looked around the court, dozens of men and women stood on the periphery of the Throne Room viewing in amazement the Cardinal's sudden and inelegant backwards flight through the air and prostration on the floor below. This would be the talk of Windsor for days to come. Not only had King Henry kicked Cardinal Peter of Saint Chrysogonus, Pope Alexander's Legate, off the platform to land on his back like a gigantic dying insect, but the king was about to ensure that war would come to the nation when his sword pierced the priest's flesh and only stopped when it hit the stone floor of the Hall.

Drawing blood from the scratch to the man's neck, the King sprayed the Cardinal's face with spittle as he screamed, "Tell that spawn of Satan in Rome, your Pope, that the King of England will not be doing his bidding a second time. Tell him this, you eminent Papal bumboy, that Henry of England may have been humbled once in order to bring peace to his nation by apologising to the Canterbury monks, but if the Pontiff dares to threaten or order me again, my armies will join with those of Spain, Portugal and Germany and unseat the filthy usurper. Then I'll ensure that he is afforded the same death as that suffered by the saints Peter and Paul! Tell Alexander that I will come to Rome in person and crucify him upside down on the banks of the Tiber. And if he dares to utter an Interdict against the people of this land, then I'll personally crucify each and every cardinal who is a member of this new College created by his predecessor, the Englishman Adrian. Tell him that, you arse-licking bed-bugging Priest, and see if your master is still brave enough to order me to accede to his demands."

Leaving him still sprawled on his back, waving his arms and legs, the Cardinal shouted, "Majesty ... please ... wait! England will not be placed under an Interdict, but unless you accede, then your continental lands and possessions, and all of the people therein, will be; they will be cast aside from the love and mercy of God and His Son Jesus."

Perhaps Henry didn't hear what the flailing Cardinal had just threatened, for his back was turned and he continued up to his throne. But Queen Eleanor, and the rest of the court, certainly heard. And in her heart, she breathed with relief that the king didn't turn and slice off the man's head for darling to utter such a threat. An impetuous thing to do, especially for one lying prone on his back.

So the king retreated up the three steps of the dais to return to his throne. Nobody minded that a cleric lost his dignity before a monarch, but the death of one so close to the Papal throne couldn't be excused.

Now they could see he'd been saved from his execution, two of the Cardinal's acolyte priests rushed to grip him by the arms and haul him back to his feet. One was tempted to brush the dust from the back of his chasuble, but quickly realised that it would only add to the Cardinal's indignity. Suddenly upright, the Cardinal was wary of climbing back up the stairs to stand as equal before the King and within reach of his fists and boots. Instead, he shook off the helping hands and stepped before the dais, looking up at the ruler of all England and half of France.

Wiping the blood off his neck with the sleeve of his cape, the Cardinal struggled to recapture the dignity of his office as well as the authority of his mission by sounding calm and authoritative, and not as he truly was, still shocked and nervous. Clearing his throat, he said, "Your Majesty, my embassy here today has nothing to do with the previous understanding between yourself and His Holiness concerning the late and beloved Archbishop Thomas a 'Becket. You and His Holiness have already agreed that in the fullness of time, you will journey in homage pilgrimage to the Holy Cathedral at Canterbury to abase yourself and beg forgiveness of the monks while they whip and bodily scourge you for your part in the murder of the saintly Archbishop, and that while being whipped you will recite a *Te Deum* and intone aloud the *apologia* His Holiness wrote especially for …"

Suddenly furious at the libel from the mouth of this cleric, Henry shouted, "I played no part in Becket's death. He was murdered by four of the magnates in my court who overheard and misconstrued my utterances of anger against the Archbishop, and tried to ingratiate themselves in my favour. He used to be my friend, a man I loved.

Yet the moment Becket returned from exile in France and landed on these shores, he continued to vomit poison against me. I warned him not to when we met in France, and I'd hoped he would have learned to remain silent. It was in anger that I spoke those words.

"And it was they, my magnates, not me, who misunderstood my private bequest to the Lord God to relieve me of the burden of this Archbishop. It was they, not I, who took themselves to Canterbury where they killed him. When I heard what these evil men had done, I donned sackcloth and ashes and fasted for three days.

"In penance of their crime, I commanded them to travel to Rome to beg forgiveness before the Pope, and he sent them on pilgrimage to Jerusalem, where hopefully they'll die along the way. Yet despite this, your lord and master the Pope says that I, the king of all England and my terrain beyond these shores, must bear both responsibility and punishment."

"That matter is in the past," the Cardinal said quickly. "It is an accord agreed upon between the Kingdom of England and the Holy See and is beyond our discussion. But through me, this day, his Holiness seeks merely to warn you ..."

The king glared at him. Fearing that he'd again leap

from his throne and do him damage, the Cardinal quickly corrected himself, and said, " ... to advise you of the dangers you face by your continued delay in signing the contract of marriage between your most beloved son Richard, and his intended bride, Alys of France, daughter of the King, Countess of Ponthieu and of the Vexin. The dangers of a Papal Interdict are very real, Highness. This child has been living here for two years, and her father, his Majesty, Louis, King of France, is complaining bitterly that no contract has been signed. He is concerned for the child's safety and her happiness. The Princess is but ten years old. She has lived in your court for two years, yet without the security of a contract ... "

Sitting back on his throne, King Henry screamed, "Louis? Concerned for the child's safety? He hasn't looked at her since the day she was born. And God damn your contracts, Priest! Young Princess Alys has greater protection in our court here in England than she does in France where King Louis surrounds himself with mumblecrusts and muckspouts and other ne'er-do-wells. And my beloved wife, Queen Eleanor of Aquitaine, has taken it upon herself to ensure the child's safety, comfort and happiness, her education and training so that she will become the right and royal wife of a Prince of the Crown."

A wave of approval sounded from the dozens of barons, earls, lords and knights, who, with their ladies, stood around the walls of the Throne Room in the castle, listening carefully to every nuance of the conversation. There was so much happening which would be discussed at great length as the most important men and women of the kingdom gathered on the steps and in the corridors of the castle to review the day's events and how they might use them to benefit their personal fortunes.

As the Cardinal straightened his robes of office, wondering what to say next, a warm morning wind blew in through the high casements which gently rustled the tapestries hung around the stone walls. King Henry reached over and picked up the goblet of wine his servant had placed on a small nearby table earlier. Refreshed, he picked up a cube of funnel cake and ate it, brushing some crumbs from the gold and blue doublet he was wearing beneath his great Chain and Seal of England. Calming down, King Henry picked up his crown and placed it on his head. A servant started to walk over to correct its position, but the king brushed the man away with a wave of the hand.

Slowly recovering from the discomfort and indignity he'd just suffered, the Cardinal determined that he wouldn't be deflected from the task given to him by the Pope. His life might end at any moment, but at least he'd be elevated to sainthood and spend eternity in the sight and protection of God and Jesus Christ. The contract would be signed during his visit, or the wrath of God would be brought down on King Henry's head, and the Pope would invoke an Interdict over the French territories of the King, separating every man, woman and child in those realms from Christ's eternal love and fatherly forgiveness. For the cardinal knew in the very depths of his soul that while Henry might be the king of his earthly domain, the Cardinal spoke for the Pope, and His Holiness spoke for God Almighty Himself in His Heavens.

"Majesty, His Holiness is aware of Queen Eleanor's relationship with the French Court; his Holiness is also aware that when King Louis of France repudiated Her Majesty, now your Queen, and annulled their marriage nineteen years ago, it is likely that animosity exists still between the House of a former husband and a present House of his former wife, which may encompass his successor's daughter, and ..."

"Nonsense, priest!" said the King. "There is no animosity between the King of France and me. We are brother kings, and he wishes his daughter to marry my son. We will be joined as kingdoms through the love of our children. And my Queen, Eleanor, was repudiated because of lies the French king was told by Eleanor's bastard enemies, which he was so stupid that he believed. Brothers we may be as kings, but he doesn't have the wit to wipe his own arse. There was no affair which his Queen was supposed to have had with her uncle Raymond while she was on Crusade in the Holy Land. Lies, Cardinal, which were unfounded and scurrilous," Henry shouted, becoming increasingly agitated by the Papal Legate's presumption.

Silently, Eleanor thought, *"And don't forget that mine was a loveless marriage which produced only girls, and no male heirs, through no failing of mine, despite giving this horse of an English king more sons than is good for him. I was always there to provide my holy French husband with womanly comforts. But rarely did he rise to my expectations, because my French king and husband was more of a monk than a man. A real man would have given me a farmyard of children. I've had eight with my English stallion, four of whom are sturdy lads. And God only knows how many more children he's spawned who grew in the bellies of other women."*

Though cautious of the English King's growing irritation, the Cardinal continued, "Lies, perhaps, your Majesty, but the King of France believed them, and after her Majesty Eleanor was expelled from the French court, she married you, Henry of England. His Holiness has concerns about the responsibilities which Eleanor has placed upon her own shoulders as a noble woman in the position of a mother to the Princess. But greater concerns have recently arisen, which have come to the attention of the Holy See. Reports have reached His Holiness's ears about the growing rifts in your majesty's relationship with Queen Eleanor, and there is talk in the courts of other nearby and brotherly nations about Her Majesty moving her court elsewhere to separate herself from your Majesty. What then for the treaty you of England and His Majesty of France signed at Montmirail, the terms of which, may I remind you, included the marriage of Alys to Richard, for which you are to receive the county of Berry between the borders of Touraine and Aquitaine.

"But if your marriage fractures and your wife establishes her own court elsewhere, Henry, then what security does the King of France have in a future marriage between his beloved daughter Alys and your young beloved son Richard. And if there is a severing of this household, where will the Princess Alys reside? In Windsor? Or London? Or Poitiers? Or Chinon? Or Fontevrault? What then of the contract? What then of Alys? Will there be a rift in England between yourself, King Henry, and your queen, Eleanor?"

Sitting nearby, Queen Eleanor quietly mumbled to herself, "*Deus Vult.*" Shaking her head silently, she prayed, "*God wills it.*"

But the Cardinal was edging closer to death with every word he uttered. Eleanor could see it in Henry's eyes. He was about to lose control again, and Eleanor knew that she had to intervene, not physically for that was too dangerous, like taunting a wounded boar, but intellectually which she knew would make her husband smile.

"Cardinal," she called out loudly. The entire court fell silent in surprise, and turned to listen to what Queen Eleanor would say. The little man turned to look at her. In flawless Latin, the Queen said, "My former husband, Louis of France, is the man about whom you and your master the Pope should have concerns. Not over this court of my much-beloved husband, Henry of England. This kingdom, under His Majesty, Henry of England, is a land which sings with joy each and every day. We are a prosperous God-loving people. But across the waves, Louis of France rules a land where discontent and hatreds flourish anew each morning with the rising of sun. May I remind you of what the Roman lawmaker Cicero wrote in his treatise *de Legibus ...salus populi suprema lex esto* ... let the good of the people be the supreme law. In my husband's heart, Cardinal, the good of his people, England, will always reign supreme over the demands of the Roman Pope. Ask the men and women of France if their lives under their King Louis are as good, and then ask the same question of the yeomen of England. That is your answer as to Princess Alys's safety."

Henry burst out laughing. "There you have it, priest! From the lips of the woman who has replaced Alys's long-dead mother. Since the moment she was born, the darling child has had no mother. Constance of Castile may have given her life, but she was never a mother to Alys because she died within days of the child's birth. This is the first true home that Princess Alys has known, with a loving mother and father, sisters and brothers. So return to Rome, Priest, and tell your master the Pope that the contract of marriage will be signed at a time and a place of my choosing. My choosing, priest! Not at the behest of that ninnycock who's arse sits astride the throne of the blessed Peter."

The court burst into applause and laughter. But not everybody was laughing.

Listening intently to every word from an upper balcony, hidden by one of the vast stone columns, was the ten-year-old Princess Alys, who held her breath so that her presence wouldn't be exposed, and so that she could hear what might become of her fate.

Since she'd arrived two years earlier from Poiteau Castle in January, cast out of her home by her father Louis in order to marry Richard, a younger son of King Henry and Queen Eleanor, she had barely seen the lad. As she left the warmth and security of France, she was in floods of tears for the entire journey to England; and since then, she had been frightened, lonely, and desperate for the love and comforts of her companions. Nor did she understand why her father the King had told her that it was her duty to join France and England in order to bring prosperity to his lands, and even to avoid war. What did she care of politics or matters of state. Never having known her mother, and with a father who rarely looked at her, all she wanted were her playmates.

When she'd arrived in England in January of that year, she was desperately cold, and the coldness had stayed in her body for months. The weather was atrocious, the castle freezing, and the only warmth came being near to the fires in her apartment. And neither was there warmth from the King of England, his sons or daughters, the court, and little enough from Queen Eleanor who was too busy fighting with King Henry, or conspiring with her sons, to pay her any heed to Alys's needs. His Majesty had lied when he told the Cardinal that she was happy and secure in the bosom of her new family. Only Rosamund made her happy. Dearest Rosamund.

Demeaning words and actions were the only things she'd come to expect from the boy she was destined to marry, Henry and Eleanor's second living son, Richard. Despite her many attempts to befriend him, Prince Richard, the nasty and silly lad with whom she was ordered by her father to spend the rest of her life, was more concerned with war than friendship. He spent every moment of his days pointedly ignoring Alys, and instead playing with his companions when he wasn't practicing with his weapons and learning the arts of sword and battle axe, lance and horse. The young Prince had recently become intensely enamoured of his new toy, a huge trebuchet given to him by the Worshipful Guild of Royal Armorers, and he would spend hour upon hour launching huge stones and sacks of turnips into the air. He was happier doing that than he was in developing a friendship with the girl who would become his bride.

Richard was only two years older than Alys, but she'd hoped that they could be companions in a world of adults; yet he'd done everything in his power to avoid her since she'd come to live in England. On the occasions when he and his entourage met her and her Ladies in Waiting in a corridor or passageway, he would invariably turn his head so he didn't have to look at her, and on occasion spit out some nasty and cutting remark, telling his giggling companions how tall and thin she was, how ugly were girls from France, how thin and spindly were her legs, or how funny was the way in which she spoke. So she spent her days alone in her apartments, continuing her education, learning the Anglo-Saxon language of the common people, and trying to determine how she could become one of the Royal family.

Sometimes Prince Richard was present when she was invited to dine in the Banqueting Hall with the court. She would be seated next to him, but as she sat, he would find an excuse to stand and go to talk with another at the table. Sometimes one of his crude and nasty friends would fill his seat and spend the entire meal either pointedly ignoring her or saying things which were deliberately hurtful. Often, she would stand, walk before the King and Queen, bow her head and curtsey politely, then leave the banquet early to retire to her apartments to spend the entire night crying inconsolably.

Because of the nature of Henry's banqueting hall, which was a mixture of jousting yard and bawdyhouse both in the day and at night, Queen Eleanor had instructed that Princess Alys should eat her meals in her apartments, accompanied by two ladies in waiting and two maidservants. Indeed, the only time she left her apartments to eat was when Eleanor ordered her appearance for an official function.

For the rest of her days, she was tutored in Latin, Greek, Grammar, Mathematics and Rhetoric by some learned priest from the University of Oxford. Since King Henry had forbidden English students from travelling to Paris as a result of the quarrel he had had with the exiled Archbishop Thomas a'Becket, the number of learned teachers had expanded in Oxford, and one who was old and wise and uninterested in women, had been appointed to her.

When she wasn't learning, she did her embroidery. On occasion, when granted permission by the Queen, she would ride with her companions through the English countryside.

But there were moments in her life which were brightened by Rosamund. As she left the balcony overlooking the Throne Room, she hoped that the beautiful Rosamund wouldn't be engaged in satisfying His Majesty, but instead would be in her apartments when she returned. Now that the interview with the Cardinal was over, and as he walked slowly backwards, refusing to bow to the King, Alys too decided that this was the right time for her to make herself invisible and return to her apartments. Her two ladies in waiting, standing in an outer corridor, asked her about the interchange with the Cardinal. They hadn't seen the Prelate being kicked down the stairs of the throne's dais, but knew something untoward was happening because of the raised voices.

Princess Alys told them briefly what had transpired, but instead of laughing, they were saddened that still no date had been set for the finalisation of the contract of marriage. But in her heart, Alys was actually pleased. In the two years that she'd been in the English court, she'd formed a very bad opinion of her future husband, the Prince Richard. As the daughter of a King, she knew that love was inevitably absent from a political marriage, but what she'd hoped for was respect, for harmony, perhaps even for admiration - if not for herself, then for her position.

She'd brought a dowry to the marriage which not only included a valuable parcel of land, but troubadours had written songs about her saying that she was beautiful, clever, bright and well-educated. Yet Richard cared not an iota for any of these qualities and had ensured that she felt a constant state of belittlement in his presence. The more she ignored his arrows of venomous words against her, the angrier and more frustrated he became, which led to his acts and insults becoming crueller and cruder.

But Rosamund understood the problems the young Princess was suffering, and hers was the shoulder on which Alys rested her head when the weight of the world became too heavy.

As they entered her apartments, Alys beamed a smile when she saw Rosamund sitting and working on some embroidery she'd left in the hoops that morning. When she heard their return, Rosamund turned, beamed a smile, and stood. She curtsied deeply, a continuous joke between them because of Rosamund's status as King Henry's mistress, and Alys's status as daughter of a King, and the future bride of a prince. Then Alys walked over, and the two hugged like older and younger sisters. Though Rosamund was nearly twenty years older than Alys, since the Princesses' arrival in the English Court, she had taken on the roles of counsellor, friend, mentor, mother and father.

"So, tell me everything, my darling. Don't dare miss out a single detail. What happened? Did the Cardinal prevail? Is the contract signed?" Rosamund asked.

Alys smiled. She loved hearing Rosamund speak the language of Northern France in her Welsh accent. And when she spoke Latin to King Henry, it was especially musical and funny.

"Well, His Majesty treated the Cardinal with all the respect that the man deserved," Alys told her.

Instantly understanding, Rosamund began to say, "Oh dear! Oh dear, dear! I suppose that meant ...".

"... it meant that Henry kicked the ridiculous little Cardinal in his belly and sent him flying half-way down the Throne Room to land on his back."

Rosamund burst out laughing. "Dear God Almighty in heaven," she said, calming herself. "Did a bolt of lightning come down from Heaven? Did the Archangel Michael suddenly appear high in the transom? So, is the contract going to be signed? Will you marry Richard?"

"Not if I can avoid it," said Alys. "He's cruel and silly and horrible. I hate him, Rosamund. I don't want to marry him. He'll treat me like a ... a ..." She struggled to think of a description of the way life would be with the Prince when he and she were old enough to marry.

Rosamund hugged the girl again, tighter this time. "Little sister," she whispered into her ear. "It's the lot of women like us to be treated in that way by the men to whom we're given by our fathers and mothers. We are nothing more than chattels in the scheme of life. And you, especially, being the daughter of a king, are of great value to your nation because of what your marriage can bring to your country ... wealth, peace, security, an end to war ..."

"But I don't want to be a chattel. I want to be loved, feel secure, respected," Alys whispered. "I don't want to be like Queen Eleanor who fights every day and night with His Majesty. I don't want to be like ..."

Her sudden embarrassed silence was filled by Rosamund, who said, "... like me? The mistress of a King. Hated by Queen Eleanor and her ladies, hated by the jealous women of the court for my access to Henry? Hated by the Archbishops and the rest of the clergy who see me as preventing their being able to whisper into

Henry's ear? Hated by the Lords and Earls and Barons and knights? And yet here I am, as I have been for years, warming the King's bed at night, staying out of sight from the rest of the court while awaiting his return from hunting, soothing his brow when his temper is inflamed. And here I will remain as the King's whore until His Majesty tires of me, or another woman catches his eye. Then I'll be cast off, sent out from here, and hope to find a man who will close his eyes to my past and want to marry me for who I am and not what I've been made."

"But it doesn't have to be like that, Rosamund," insisted Alys. "Your own beloved father, Lord Walter de Clifford of the Welsh Marches was in love with your mother Margaret. You told me so yourself. And when you first met King Henry, when your father served in his Majesty's campaign in Wales, against the wishes of your family, he favoured you and took you away from your home. Your father denied his King, until he was threatened. So why couldn't my father have done that for me? Why did he have to parcel me up like a haunch of pork and send me to this cold and horrible land?"

"You poor child," Rosamund said, stroking Alys's long blond hair. "Don't compare yourself to me, I beg you. You know what they say of me. They play with my name; one moment I'm *Rosa Mundi* …"

"*Rosa* …? Forgive me, sister," said Alys, "but my Latin is not yet as good as yours."

The older woman smiled, and kissed Alys on the forehead. "Rosa Mundi means the rose of the world. But when they speak behind my back in passageways where they don't think I can hear them, the nature of the men and especially the ladies of the court changes. For then I am no longer Rosamund or even Rosa Mundi. The next moment, to their laughter and ridicule, I'm *Rosa Immunda,* which means the unclean rose. Sometimes, the clerics of the Court whisper another name under their smelly breath, I become *Rosa Immundi,* and that, dearest Alys, means they're calling me the unchaste rose. A whore; a harlot; a fallen woman.

"They think it's funny, but it's like a dagger in my heart. I was a virgin when Henry first saw me and he's the only man I've ever known. I had no choice but allow him to have knowledge of my body. And now in their eyes, and those of the rest of the world, I'm a fallen woman. Yes, child, my parents loved me, but in the years since I was made Henry's mistress, they have not once written or sent messages. Henry won't allow me to send a messenger to my home in Wales, in case it causes my father to demand my return or a vast payment for his defiling of me; but his real fear is that my father will raise his army and march out of Wales to reclaim me. Yet still they remain silent since I left my home. In truth, dearest Alys, I think it's because my father recognises my reduced value to him and looks towards my sisters for his future."

Alys shook her head. "I don't understand."

Rosamund smiled and kissed the girl again on her forehead. "My value to my father comes from my chastity. It is the only thing of value a woman can possess. A woman no longer chaste is diminished in value, and can't hope to attract a husband of worth, such as a Duke or an Earl. Now I am fallen, I'm certain that my father's eyes are closed to me forever as I am no longer of any value to him. I keep reassuring Henry that he should have no fears concerning my father's intentions to reclaim me. I've told him that in my father's eyes, I am of less value than an old pair of boots. It's as though I've died in my father's heart."

"But why not tell King Henry of what the Lords and Ladies of the court do to you? Say about you? Why suffer this abuse when you are the love of his life. You should be revered, respected. You're the King's favourite," said Alys plaintively.

"If I tell the King what his courtiers are saying behind my back, he'll draw his sword and hack a dozen men to death in his fury. And when he's calm and has forgotten the insults against me, what will that mean for me? I'll be the woman who caused the death of clerics and other men of God. If he kills a Duke or a Baron, I'll be that family's enemy for all eternity. They will ensure that my life becomes a living Hell on earth. But your life, dearest little sister, is destined to be different. Oh Alys, I envy you so greatly. As the future bride of a Prince of the realm, you will ride through towns and villages and hold your head high in pride. You're to be a member of the Royal family. You're to marry a Prince of England and Normandy, of Aquitaine and God only knows what other lands which Henry will conquer. And with every breath in your body, you will be a mere death or two away from succeeding to become Queen of England. Think of that, Alys, as the life which God Almighty has carved in rock for you because of your birth, and not of the misery your life is at this moment."

The young girl pulled away, reached up and kissed Rosamund on the cheek, and then crossed herself, praying to God that her beloved older sister was correct.

Part the SECOND

In which Queen Eleanor of Aquitaine gathers her children to her French court, in order to plan the overthrow of her husband, old King Henry, and install her children as rulers of their own lands.

———◆———

Poitiers Castle Aquitaine, central France Salle des Pas Perdu 20th, April 1173

Tall, majestic, thirteen-year-old Princess Alys of France, Countess of Ponthieu, future wife of Prince Richard, trailed after Queen Eleanor, desperate to keep up with the fleet-footed forceful woman. Obligated to carry her own bags by an order to his servants from Prince Richard, she looked in anger and frustration at her future husband and his brother Prince Geoffrey, walking swiftly in their mother's footsteps, hastening to reach the end of the Hall. It was easy for them, as they were unburdened by their baggage which was being carried in the rear by their servants. As they walked into the vast gallery, they chatted amiably with each other. It was another aspect of the cruelty which the sixteen-year-old Richard showed towards his future bride. Nor did his brother, Geoffrey, a year younger and even less mature, consider the young princesses' plight.

Alys was confident that if Eleanor had turned her back and seen what was happening, she would have berated the servants, snapped her fingers, and Alys would have been freed of her burdens. Though she and Queen Eleanor were growing increasingly distant because of the often-outrageous compliments which King Henry would often pay Alys, compliments she neither expected nor welcomed, none-the-less, Eleanor always behaved like a queen, and would insist that a young women, the daughter of a king, didn't carry her own baggage.

But at the moment, Eleanor was too concerned about returning to the Castle, and especially anxious to know what how the plans were developing for the young King Henry to overthrow his father, old King Henry.

As they walked deeper into the astoundingly cavernous hall known as the *Salle des Pas Perdu*, Alys quickly understood why it was known as the hall of lost footsteps. As they walked their footsteps didn't echo back to them, but were lost in the vastness of the space. Nor did the huge fire blazing away in the carved fireplace at the distant end of the hall even come close to warming the chill in the April air.

The others didn't seem to notice the cold in the hall. Eleanor was intent on reaching the banquet table at the far end, closer to the fire, when it had been arranged that she'd be greeted by young King Henry. Though he was brother to Richard, at eighteen, he was two years older, and was the only one of Eleanor's sons who treated her with something approaching warmth.

For Alys, it continued to be a mystery that King Henry had elevated his oldest son young Henry to be co-equal regent. Understanding the tensions within royal families, she knew that a son ignored was like a fire brand dipped in pitch, one which could ignite a conflagration if left unattended. So it was told that the old king had allowed his eldest son and heir to the throne to acquire the title 'king' in order to avoid the hideous family rivalry and quarrels which always threatened to rip apart the royal household; but when the son wanted some of the powers from his father, powers which he wanted to exercise and which were the rite of the title, yet the old king refused to cede any to the young king, his move was quickly seen to be a symbolic deception.

Young Henry had left England in a state of fury and for some time had lived in the Palace of the King of France. Now he was come to Poitiers to meet with his mother, the world's most powerful woman, in order to determine how he should proceed.

But knowing Eleanor as well as she did, Alys knew that old King Henry's queen would treat the young king of England not like a King, but a son. She had no intention of being other than a Queen and a mother; a Queen to a living monarch and mother to a living monarch. Alys knew that Eleanor had no intention of curtseying to her son, whose honorific title had been bestowed on him four years ago. Surely old King Henry must have known that bestowing such a meaningless elevation would fail in its one objective. Yet he had underestimated both young Henry and his wife Eleanor.

Which was proven because the continuous hatreds and animosities continued, and quelling future rebellion hadn't succeeded. Young Henry's fury grew because as titular king, he was like a stallion smelling mares in heat, yet firmly tethered in his stall.

As Alys paced towards the warmth and food waiting for the new arrivals at the far end of the Hall, she wondered where the past years of her life had disappeared. Were the five humiliating, debilitating and demeaning years of her life since being sent to England, simply wasted? From the tender age of eight, when she'd been playing happily in her home in France to be suddenly plucked up as if she was a mote of dust in a windstorm, and dropped *holus-bolus* into the most relentless, fractious, irritable and restless families in all the world, had been a living trauma which continued without ease.

Now she was travelling with Her Majesty Queen Eleanor to Aquitaine, with her sons Richard and Geoffrey and John. Did the old King know? He and Eleanor were long estranged, and it was known far and wide that since she'd established a separate court from the old King, she was always using her sons to her advantage, and against her husband.

But when old Henry discovered what Queen Eleanor was plotting, for surely she was plotting something, would he raise his army, travel south from England, and massacre his entire family? And would she, a young thirteen-year-old, be considered by the old King to be a conspirator, even one of the planners of the plot, and be put to death, just as surely as would Queen Eleanor once Henry's anger was roused? Would old Henry execute young Henry, his heir? His other sons? Would he execute Richard, her fiancé? Geoffrey and John? If so, then which Plantagenet would be left alive to rule once old Henry was dead and buried? Surely not the daughters of Henry and Eleanor, Matilda, young Eleanor or Joanna, all now queens in their own right of monarchs in Saxony, Castille and Sicily! Nor would the Barons ever accept a woman as sole monarch over a nation which, should war occur between the young and old kings, would leave the nation fractious, even warlike, as rivals looked hungrily at the power of an empty throne, and fought for succession.

But old King Henry did have two brothers, Geoffrey the Count of Nantes and William FitzEmpress, all sons of the old queen, the Empress Matilda. Yet knowing the mood of the nobility of England, neither would they be accepted by the Barons and Earls who would be asked to swear fealty? Would the nobles of England and Aquitaine accept one or other of them as their king? Surely not. They might be siblings of old Henry, but neither had set foot in England, even once.

Which meant that if old Henry did march south with his army, then Young King Henry would have to raise an army in response, and meet him in Le Havre. And it would be a bloody battle. There would be many dead and wounded, and much ransom to be paid for the nobility who were captured. And later that afternoon, and all through the following day, when the crows and ravens had had their fill of dead men's eyes, then the *scawageours* and rummagers would descend on the field of battle from nearby towns to steal purses of money, swords and daggers and any other valuables which the dead on longer needed in this life.

Alys's only hope for a future where her life was happy, would be for Eleanor to insist that her fiancé, Prince Richard, second in line to the throne, took control of the army instead of young King Henry in order to lead the troops into battle against his father. And if Almighty God was on her side, then Richard would be killed in battle, and she would become free to return to her father and the safety of her French home.

But the moment she looked towards the movement which suddenly occurred at the end of the hall, Alys knew in her heart that young King Henry would never allow his younger brother Richard to take over the duty of a king and to lead the fight against their father. When he appeared from an antechamber, he was already dressed in the armour of war. His chest covered in a gleaming cuirass emboldened with the emblems of the House of Plantagenet, the three lions *passant guardant*. Yet the young king's head, arms and legs were free of armour, and he walked towards his mother Eleanor, and bowed low in respect.

"Welcome, Queen of England and Aquitaine and Mother to your people," he shouted as she neared him.

Acknowledging his filial welcome, Eleanor held out her hand so that Henry could grasp it and kiss her ring. Then she embraced him like a mother. Soon, they were joined by Richard, John and Geoffrey.

"John? You've come? With our brothers? I'm not surprised by your presence, Richard and yours, Geoffrey, but John? Your being here is a surprise. I assumed that you'd remain in England in order to lick our father's boots," Henry said.

"I'm here because mother insisted," the seven-year-old lad said, trying to sound as adult as he could before his brothers. "Mother said I had to come, and couldn't stay with my father. But it wasn't a request, it was command. She said that events are afoot and that my place is with my brothers and not with my father. She forced me to come. England, mother says, isn't a place for Plantagenets at the moment, until things become more clear," said Prince John.

Sensing the beginning of a quarrel, Eleanor said swiftly, "Be that as it may, John, when events play out, your place is beside me, your mother, and your brothers. You're still very young, and your father will not treat you well if my plans play out to my desires.

"My warning was very real. If you stand beside your father, then the executioner's vengeful sword will descend twice, not just once, and your neck will be one of those to be severed. So, my sons, let us discuss our future moves; but before we talk strategy, let's eat and drink. I've had nothing since crossing the borders of my land," said Eleanor, walking past her group of children towards the banqueting table, and closer still to the fire. Stopping at the table, she picked up a large round trencher made from stale bread and placed slices of ham, duck and chicken onto it along with two pies, one made with mushrooms and the other with spinach, before she collected two hunks of fresh bread from the pannier. As she skirted the table to get to the chairs arranged around the fireplace, she picked up both a knife, as well as one of the new double-pronged implements introduced recently from Florence to skewer meat in order to carry it to the mouth. As she sat, a servant poured her a goblet of red wine and placed it on the arm of her seat.

Ignoring Alys, who by this time had reached the table and was still carrying the two satchels of her baggage, the sons took their bread trenchers, placed a pile of food on top, and joined their mother around the fireplace. Alys, just as cold and hungry, put down the baggage, and placed slices of meats, small pies and mushrooms on her trencher. She was about to carry it to the fireplace to take her seat with her family when she realised that every chair had been filled. So she left her bags near to the table, and found a seat close to one of the walls. But she could still hear what was being said.

"Remember, my sons, that when you've finished your meal, it is a custom of the nobility of Aquitaine that the trenchers we use and their meat juices are collected and given to the poor who wait for our largess at the servants' portico," Eleanor said.

All of her sons dutifully nodded, until Prince John asked, "They eat the trencher? The stale bread?"

"Sometimes it's their only food for the week, and much prized," Eleanor explained. "As the Royal family, it is our responsibility to protect our citizens. Ensuring that they don't starve is one way."

John, her youngest son, shook his head. "But I've been as trainee page to other courts, and nobody gives away the trenchers to the people. They throw them out for the pigs. Why do ...?"

Eleanor said sternly, "My sons. May I remind you all of what the great Pericles of Athens said to his people ... *Our government does not copy our neighbours, but is an example to them.* In so many ways, the Kingdom of England and Aquitaine is the very model of greatness because of the way we treat our people. And giving our used trenchers to the poor is not the only way in which we're different. It is also another tradition of the Dukedom of Aquitaine that the women of this land are allowed liberties unknown through the rest of the world. We women, both of the Court and the towns, may freely engage in conversation with men without the need first to be introduced; we women may indulge in discussions of political and state and religious matters without deferring to a husband or father; and most precious of all, we may be in the presence of a man without the need of a chaperone while always remembering our rank and the decorum with which we were born.

"So if a lady of this Dukedom comes up to you and engages you in conversation without first being invited and with no man present, don't be shocked or surprised, for if you reject her, the damage to reputation will be yours, and not hers," said Eleanor.

Alys listened carefully, and on impulse, shouted out, "Then your Majesty, as a woman now in Aquitaine, and a woman who has been part of this family since I was eight, may I be permitted to join your assembly and sit by the fire in order to eat?"

In surprise, the sons, as well as Eleanor, turned to see from where the voice had just emanated, the young voice of a woman which had interrupted the family meeting. Spotting her on a seat by the stairs which led to an upper balcony, Eleanor said, "Dear God, child. I had no idea you were there. Why are you sitting over there in the cold? Draw near beside the fire and join your family."

The Queen snapped her fingers at a servant and ordered him to carry the Princess Alys's seat over and place it in front of the fire. With a look of command, Eleanor indicated to her sons Richard and Geoffrey that they should move their seats apart so Princess Alys could sit between them in the family's semi-circle around the blazing logs. Geoffrey immediately complied, but the Queen had to signal a silent glare of command to a recalcitrant Richard before he rose in a surly fashion and shifted his chair so that his fiancée had room to sit with her future family. Politely, the young Princess turned to Geoffrey, then Richard, and thanked them for their courtesy.

When all were seated and comfortable and warmed by the fire, Queen Eleanor turned, and with a snap of her fingers, ordered all of the servants to leave the hall. It was a move which surprised her children. An atmosphere of gravity and secrecy suddenly descended on the family. Matters of state were about to be discussed in the absence of the old King, which evidenced that aspect of her nature for which their mother was known throughout the kingdoms of England and Portugal, France and Spain, Germany and Italy … conspiracy!

"This Hall has many ears within its four walls, and so I will speak softly so that we're not overheard. What I say today will be held to your bosoms and not divulged to any person, for any reason, until the events which I intend to put into effect take on a life and potency of their own. Swear this to me, my sons, on the hilts of your swords?" she said.

They all withdrew their swords from scabbards and lifted them to their lips. Then young King Henry and Richard kissed the sword where the cross-guard met the grip, but John and his brother Geoffrey instead kissed the sword's pommel. As one, each son said, "By the sacred blood of Christ, and by my very life, I swear it."

As they were replacing their swords, Richard looked menacingly at Alys, and said, "And what oath will you make to our mother, little Princess? Where do your loyalties lie? To the Pope? The King of France? The King of England? Or the Queen who sits before you?"

All the brothers turned and looked at Alys, who felt her face flush with both shock at the sudden confrontation, and the demeaning challenge her future husband had just made.

"My loyalties? You question my loyalties, Sir, despite that I am engaged to the son of this Queen? I'm pleased you asked, my Lord, because these loyalties on which you've just sworn by your life, lie with the family to whose ranks I have just been invited to sit. I now am, and have been since I was a babe, beside Her Majesty Queen Eleanor. My loyalties, Sir, lie with my future husband, yourself, who has shown me such tenderness and love, devotion and kindness, fidelity and fealty since I arrived in England as an eight year old child. My loyalties, Prince Richard, are to the oath I swore when your father's Royal Chaplain made me kneel before you and your father and willingly forsake all others if you will take me as your wife. Those, my Lord, my Prince Richard, are where my loyalties lie. Doubt my loyalties, and you doubt the very structure on which our lives will intertwine when we are wed."

Prince Richard's lips contracted into a thin line of fury, and he was about to utter a venomous condemnation of her defence, when instead of remaining silent, Alys suddenly continued, "But where are your loyalties, Prince Richard? To your beloved father whom you are about to stab in the back? To your beloved mother, into whose presence you had to be dragged like beaten dog? To your brother and overlord young King Henry, whom you have sworn to overthrow as co-equal ruler with your father, in those moments of your drunken honesty? To Prince Geoffrey and Prince John who you see as nothing more than footmen to do your bidding? So before you demand to know my loyalties, my Lord Prince, my future husband, answer a simple question … where are your loyalties?"

A silence descended on the Hall, broken only by the occasional crackling from the logs on the fire. Stunned by her public insolence, Richard was about to re-draw his sword and run her through, when the silence was further fractured as Queen Eleanor started to laugh, and then clap her hands in appreciation of what her future daughter-in-law had just said.

"Dear God in His Heaven, Alys, but I've underestimated you," she called out, still laughing. "I've ignored you since you came from France to become my daughter and hadn't realised that you've grown into both a beauty, and a feisty women. For one so young, you speak greater truth than Jesus when he delivered his sermon on the mount. You are welcome to sit at this family meeting, my dear, and never again will your loyalty be questioned. Take note, Richard, or ignore this woman at your peril. Dare to question her loyalty again, and she'll tie you up in silken threads of words.

"Now, my sons … and my daughter … gather closer, for things must be said for your knowledge, and yours alone." They all put down the used trenchers, and pulled their chairs close to their mother, so that if she whispered, they would be the only people able to hear.

"John, you are here for your protection from what is about to happen. As a child, you can have no part in these coming wars, but sit and listen to my counsel and that of your older brothers. Your place is beside me, your mother, because of your youth; not beside your father. Put him out of your mind.

"My sons, I have returned to Aquitaine," she said, "in order to establish once more my court. I do not intend to return to England. And it is my desire that you, my children, remain with me. Though you all have your lives to live, the next many months will be critical, and most important is that we, the wife and children of King Henry, remain together."

John sat scowling and was on the verge of tears. He wanted to return to England, to his father but his mother had just forbidden him to leave. He would have to sneak away. But instead of crying, his thoughts were interrupted when his older brother Richard suddenly spoke.

"And for what reason, Mother? Why do you want us to remain here?" asked Richard.

Instead, young King Henry answered, looking at his mother, "because our Mother Queen intends to rouse the noblemen of Aquitaine and Normandy, as well as England, to rise up against our father, King Henry. Isn't that correct, your Majesty? You're going to tell them that he's become a tyrant and must be overthrown. But the truth is that you want to secure our legacy, which means securing your own.

"And when you do raise armies in England and Aquitaine, and he's overthrown, who will replace him as ruler? Will it be me, Mother, the rightful heir and co-ruler with old King Henry. Am I to be king in this scheme of yours, Mother, for who but me could be king? I am, by the grace of God, right-royally anointed King, just and lawful ruler by primogenitor, by title and by the oath I swore? Or will the ruler of England and Wales, Aquitaine and other lands and realms, be you, Mother?"

She looked at him sternly, and said, "You! It will be you, King Henry. You will be King and Lord of these realms, by right of birth and primogenitor, yours by right of the title which was bestowed upon you before your time, and yours because of the grace of God and the solemn oath you took when you and my husband became joint rulers of these lands." Now she was no longer whispering, but had risen from her chair, facing her oldest son directly, her face flushed red with anger, her finger pointed at her son's heart.

Unintimidated by his mother's stance, Henry said calmly, "But that wasn't what I asked you, Mother. I asked who will replace King Henry as ruler when he's overthrown? Yes, it will be me, but will I be King and ruler by divine right, or just a regent for the real power who sits behind the throne? Will I simply be the man who sits atop the throne like an empty sack of turnips? Will I be king in name only as I am now, when I have a title, but everybody knows that it is old Henry who truly has the power, and rules. Or when he's rotting in Hell, will I be King, but you become the ruler of the lands? Will yours be the voice heard from my throne?"

All of those still seated looked at Henry in amazement for daring to confront a woman of Eleanor's power. But he had, and now he would see whether his move was one of wisdom or stupidity.

"I have passed my fiftieth year, Henry. I'm an old woman. Women rarely reach my age, having already died from exhaustion these past fifteen years. I'm alive by the grace of the Almighty and knowing how to navigate the murderous tides of a turbulent royal sea. My sole ambition, and I address this to all my sons, to you, Richard and you, Geoffrey and you, John, and especially you, Henry, is that you all remain powerful and strong and healthy during the next year or more when great troubles will be brought to our kingdoms, and that you succeed to the offices and stations of life to which Almighty God has appointed you. There will be war coming, my sons. War between father and sons. War between those noblemen who side with us, who see their future in our courts, and against those nobility who don't believe that we will succeed and remain by Henry's side. War which will tear nations apart. War will be looked at closely by our enemies to see how they can take advantage of two sides engaged in fighting. War is beautiful and terrible, my sons, and we should welcome it like ripe fruit, and dread it like poison. And to answer your question, Henry, as to whether I will be the power behind the throne, the answer my son, is no.

"For over twenty years, I have counselled the King, advised him, whispered guidance into his ears, but at all times I devoted myself only as the loving and dutiful queen, respectful of the majesty of the King. Many years ago, he took my advice, but today he shuns me and will not hear my voice.

"In those days, he was young and inexperienced, his mind was well learned, but his thought were more of hunting and bedding girls than bearing the weight of the Crown. But I was not as young, not concerned with matters other than kingship, and had already born the weight of a crown. I had been the daughter and wife of kings, and knew Kingship better than I knew any other aspect of my life. I was already thirty years of age when I married Henry, who was a young buck of just nineteen tender years. I brought with me to the marriage a great inheritance, these lands of France. Which was what his accursed brother Count Geoffrey of Nantes wanted when he heard that King Louis, Alys's father, had annulled me. Yes, Geoffrey, Henry's brother, knew of my great beauty and desired me for himself, but he really wanted to marry me to acquire my lands of Aquitaine.

"You all know the story, but for the sake of my daughter Alys, I'll tell you again. I had just escaped, and was riding away from my former husband, the King of France, when Henry's brother Geoffrey heard of my journey. So he tried to kidnap me when I was on the road. My only thought was to ride away from my former husband, Louis and the annulment he had just created. The idea that a man would dare to kidnap me, a queen, never occurred. So when I knew I was in danger from Geoffrey, I had to write urgently to his brother Henry and ask him to marry me and save me from that madman."

Suddenly, Richard interrupted, and said, "we know all of this mother. It is our family history. It is the song of the Troubadour. Alys can learn this at another time."

"Silence," she ordered. "There is much untold, and until you learn all of the facts of my life and that of old King Henry, you cannot begin to understand the true cause for which I called this meeting of you, my children.

"My marriage to my first husband, the French King, was annulled because there was no male issue. Just two daughters. But more than that, it was all to do with the interference of Saint Bernard of Clairvaux who whispered into my husband's ears that I was nothing more than a whore and strumpet, who had become the lover of my uncle while in the Holy Land. Lies, of course, but my French husband was in a lifelong religious frenzy and had become more priest than real man. He was in perpetual awe of Bernard. So at the urging of that damned priest, my husband King threw me out. Because of that accursed Bernard, that man, that saint. Such a hideous parody of the Son of God. He even denounced the wonderful Peter Abelard, the greatest thinker of this age, just because he tried to bring rational thought to the understanding of the Bible. May Bernard rot in the hottest fires of hell for his accursed mouth.

"And I arrived in England, and when I told your father of the role Bernard had played in King Louis' decision to annul me, he burst out laughing. It was just the sort of scandal he wanted to hear and used it as revelry with all of his friends. From that moment onward, I loved him. We waited only eight weeks to get married. But from the second night of our acquaintance when I first arrived in

England, we were as man and wife.

"And by God, could he make my body sing. On the night of our marriage, even though he'd known me every night since my arrival, your father entered me eight times, and before sunrise in the morrow, while I could barely move, he and his groomsmen were able to jump atop their mounts and bring home ten brace of pheasant, a boar and a deer for the wedding breakfast. We loved each other with a fierce passion, even when he thrust his manhood into my Ladies in Waiting. But I knew that it was just the desires of his young body, for his heart was mine and mine alone. And we would still love each other had it not been for his appetite for the Welsh whore who still warms his bed, despite my best entreaties to rid the palace of her.

"But that is all a prelude to my answer to your question, my son, an explanation of what I am about to say. Will I be the power behind your throne, King Henry? No, by my solemn pledge and troth. I have only one fight left in me, and that is to see the crown given to you, not in name with some promise which vanishes like the mists of the morning, but by God-given right of Kingship. Will I advise you? Yes, as would any mother when she sees her son about to incur a mistake. Will my word be law? No!

Not now, not ever! As a grand dame, as a Queen Mother, it is my desire to retire to this, the lands of my inheritance, and live out whatever years God decides to grand me, and pray for the success of my beloved children," she said, picking up the goblet of wine and sipping it.

Henry looked at Eleanor, then his brothers, then Princess Alys, and awaited the reaction. It came swiftly. And surprisingly! The reaction came not from young King Henry, but from his brother Prince Richard. Suddenly in the silence of the Hall, as her words disappeared into the vast empty space, Richard burst out laughing. Geoffrey and John looked at him in shock. But Henry, as well as Princess Alys, both understood the reason for his mirth, and the venom which was behind it. Richard's laughter continued, and grew louder, exacerbated when he began to applaud. Henry, too, started to laugh.

"I'm pleased that you find what I said was amusing, my princely son Richard. Could you share your amusement with the others, because I fear that you're the only one who found what I said to be funny," Queen Eleanor said archly.

Still laughing, Richard said, "What a wonderful tale you weave, mother. What imaginative tapestries you entwine for us all to gaze upon. You've just created a drape in the most beautiful colours of Nature, blues and greens and yellows, all threads blended by you into a picture of peaceful and harmonious coexistence. In this picture, my Queen and Mother, Old Henry is lying, headless, at the bottom of the tapestry, his bloodless body being eaten by carrion birds, while above him in the picture sits you, surrounded by your children, and above you, wearing his crown and sitting on his throne, is my beloved brother, young King Henry.

"Wonderful, what a picture. What a tapestry. Perfect in every way, except that you've left some important characters out of your design. Perhaps you didn't have enough thread. You've omitted to include Morgana la Fay, the evil fairy, written about recently by Geoffrey of Monmouth. Well, Mother, where, in this tapestry you've just woven in front of our eyes, is the fairy Morgana? And Merlin the Wizard? Where is he? For how else will you achieve your magic of keeping your nose and fingers out of the business of kingship without the help of a fairy or a witch or a wizard?" he said.

At the mention of these beings, of fairies and wizards and witches from the world of spirits, the other brothers crossed themselves.

Richard continued, "You've woven a spell, and expect

your sons to meekly become your playthings. I was expecting you to quote the words of Saint Augustine, *"Lord, help me to be pure, but just not yet."* Well, your purity may speak to my young and naïve brothers, but not to me, Mother, and not Henry! You might be able to fool my gullible brother Geoffrey, and you'll certainly fool my young and stupid little brother John, but neither Henry nor I are unfamiliar with your wiles, and we see through your web of lies. You say that you were merely a counsellor to our father. That you were nothing more than his boon companion, his bed mate, his cloth to wipe his brow.

"Yet it is known throughout the land that in the early days of your marriage, while he was on horseback visiting his realm and dispensing justice, you remained at home, and arbitrated in disputes ... disputations between Barons and Earls, between Yeomen and Knights and overseers and serfs; disputations which were brought to you over land and taxes and dues to the Crown. You presided as judge over many of the courts, while administering the revenues due to the King. It's also said that those who came to find justice and found you as their judge were horrified by your cruel and impetuous decisions."

Unperturbed by his usual insults, it was only then

that Geoffrey understood why his brothers Henry and Richard found Queen Eleanor's speech to them so funny. John, being only seven, understood virtually nothing of what was being said.

Alys looked at Eleanor and saw that she was about to rain down all the furies of Hell against her son Richard, causing a rupture which this family could ill-afford at this juncture. Unity was essential for her as a future wife of Richard, and for the hopes of peace between the family.

So unexpectedly, Alys said, "My good Lord Richard, as a daughter of this family, I have a right to speak. Your beloved mother, Queen Eleanor, has lived the life of a dutiful wife to two Christian kings since she was a girl. Her Majesty knows what is right and proper in a wife ... and in a Queen. Not once has she given reason to distrust her motives with old King Henry and nor do I believe that she will seek other than the status of advisor to young King Henry when he sits on the throne. Throughout Christendom, Kings and Cardinals work together for the good of their peoples. Why should it be different for the wife ... or the mother ... of a king? I have lived with Queen Eleanor as her daughter since I was a child of eight, and though I was very young, I witnessed in her eyes and her heart the love and devotion of a wife to a husband, a mother to her children …"

Richard turned, and hissed, "Be silent, girl! Do not dare to interfere in matters which don't concern you. You have nothing to say here in this assemble of English Royals. You are nothing more to me and this family than a sack of French grain. You will remain silent while we, the nobility and mighty of the English nation, discuss our future."

As though a castle wall had just been breached, Alys suddenly felt all of her anger and bile erupting. She could feel the revulsion, the belittling of five years of life with the Plantagenets rise up in her gorge and threaten to choke her.

For the first time since they'd met when she was eight, she raised her voice and allowed her anger to flow from her to fill the room. "How dare you speak to me like that, Richard? How dare you order me to be silent when I sit with my brothers and my mother about to discuss my family's future? My family, Richard, as well as yours. Since I first arrived in this family, you have done everything in your power to dismiss, to belittle and to nullify me. I am destined to be your future wife, yet you insult me every day in public, ignore me in private, ridicule me to your friends, mock and disparage me to any audience who will give you their ear, and cast me into the furthest recesses of your life.

"And how have I responded to these insults, thrusts and blows? Like the true lady I am. Not once, husband to be, have I denied your sovereignty, nor decried you, nor ridiculed or spoken evil of you. I have always treated you with the reverence due to a Prince of the Realm, which is more than the way you have treated me as a Princess of France, as the daughter of a King.

"This is my family, Prince Richard, and if you deny that, then nullify our contract of marriage, and I shall return to my family in France. For doubt this not, my Lord ... when I leave your house, you should prepare for war, for that is without doubt what will be the reaction against you when my father and the French people learn of the grievous insults by which you assail me," she said. "Insult me one more time, Richard, and I return to France, deny our contract of marriage, and war will come to England."

Richard's mouth transformed into a snarl, and he was about to scream insults in answer of her, until Queen Eleanor suddenly stood and moved closer to the fire, he remained silent. And as silence dawned on all the group, all eyes were on the Queen to determine what would be said next. Would she defend her son against Alys's insults, or would she stand beside Alys?

Suddenly feeling less secure, Richard just sat there, stunned that Alys had the temerity to have raised her voice against him before his family, and said such things; Henry worried that this could cause a further rupture in such uncertain times for the family; and Geoffrey and John delighted in the reproach their brother Richard had just suffered.

Eleanor turned and looked at all her children, one by one. Then she centred her glare on Alys and Richard. "There will be no more talk of your returning to the King of France, my daughter Alys. There will be no talk of abrogating your marriage to Richard. You are a beloved daughter of this family, due all the entitlements and privileges bestowed upon you by your right of birth, and in that estate, you will remain in this Court as long as I breathe.

"But as to you, Prince Richard, there will be no future insults or offences against this lady Princess, your future wife. Such talk will cease immediately. Alys, since she came to us as a child, has shown herself at all times to be loving, respectful, and dear to our hearts. To treat her as you do, Richard, shows that you're blind to her value. She came into this family, not just to England, as a dove of peace between our Kingdoms and France, not just for the bounty of land and trade which came with her person as dowry, but as a beautiful, passionate and commendable young woman ... a woman of dignity, standing and worth. Open your eyes, you foolish boy, and see the gem which your father, as well as fortune, has placed in your hands."

Then she addressed the family. Despite the continued feelings of anger, she lowered her voice so that she couldn't be heard beyond those who surrounded her. "Now we will put aside our petty jealousies and disputes, and for once and all times, we will be a family, together. We have, you and I, a common enemy in your father and my husband, King Henry. He has ruled his lands well since he became King, but that is no longer true. Today he is gravely weakened. The Lords of Aquitaine, of Normandy, of Anjou, of England and Wales are divided in their loyalties, and their division is growing by the day.

"Old King Henry spends more time lying in his bed, being kept warm and amused by his mistress Rosamund, than attending to the affairs of the nation. Divisions are growing every day on the borders and the dissent is spreading like a plague into the cities. Nor are there

Lords and nobles more querulous and fractious than the noblemen of England who are always on the edge of revolt. But while once they were cowered by his might, today that might has diminished, because the Pope commanded that he be forced to crawl on his hands and his knees along the cold stony steps of Canterbury Cathedral where he was stripped naked before the monks of that Abbey, and whipped while singing a Te Deum and reciting some *apologia* written by the Pope.

"The King, your father, was humiliated before all England because of his part in the death of Thomas Becket, and much of the rock on which his Majesty once stood has now crumbled into dust and he has been brought low. This means that in the eyes of the Earls and Barons, Lords and Knights, he is severely weakened as a ruler and a King. And because of his overt weakness, the rulers of nearby lands, Scotland and Norway and many others, are looking at England, and wondering whether to invade.

"His weakness for him is a terrible thing, but for us offers an opportunity, a chance, as though Almighty God has unlocked the gates of the Kingdom and opened the future for you, my sons.

"Henry, you asked what role I would play when your

father had been brought low. Simply this, my son. I wish to reclaim my inheritance and have Aquitaine returned to me. Though you will hold suzerainty over the Duchy of Aquitaine, I will rule independently, while paying you my tributes and taxes. Here I will rule as Duchess...as Queen Dowager...the title is yours to provide, my son Henry. But I will leave England and return to the land of my birth," she said.

Turning to Richard, she said, "and as for you, my son Richard, as second in line to the throne, you and your bride to be, Alys, will rule this land of Aquitaine, which is in suzerainty to England. You and Alys will remain here with me, after the war against your father, which will determine the succession, and you will rule this land with me. And when I die, you will be sovereign, though with King Henry of England, your brother, as your overlord. As to the title, we will accommodate your rank and position as Prince of the Realm and son of a king. Alys, your title will remain Princess as a result of your birth; but after my death, you may become Queen of Aquitaine, with your brother Henry's permission."

Then she set her eyes on Geoffrey. "You, Geoffrey, who always wanted your own army, well, with your brother King Henry's permission, defeat the current incumbents and become King of Wales or even of Scotland, or perhaps even Ireland should you decide to conquer that land. To conquer these nations, you will raise a mighty army, but that army while on English soil, may owe deference to you as its commander, and but it will pay full allegiance to your brother Henry as King. And that, my sons, is the reason you are joining with me to overthrow your father Henry and secure your kingdoms."

They all sat back in their seats, letting the grand scheme she had just outlined sink into their minds. Out of the fog and mists they had left in England, out of an insecure and uncertain future for their family, suddenly their brilliant mother had just painted a path forward which satisfied the most base desires of them all.

All, that is, except the young Prince John, who continued to sit there with a frown on his face. Never capable of restraint or composure, he burst out, "But what about me, Mother? You've given Henry all of England, Richard now has Aquitaine, and Geoffrey has Scotland or Ireland … but what do I get? What is my Kingdom? Where will I rule? It's not fair. They get kingdoms and I get nothing. Why am I left out? It isn't fair. I'm always forgotten. You always put me last. Why aren't I being given a land to rule. I'm born a Prince and I should be given a land over which to be King."

As he spoke, his voice broke, as though he was about to start to cry. Alys looked at him in amazement. In all the time she'd known him, he'd taunted her, following Richard's instructions and belittled her, and acted like little more than a child in her company. She'd never felt comfortable with him, and his pathetic selfish outburst now showed how utterly incapable he would be as a king.

Then Alys glanced at her future husband, Richard. He was smirking, unable to hold his true feelings from showing on his face. Perhaps he was smiling because at last he would be a King, even of a land called Aquitaine held by his older brother. Perhaps he was smirking because of the distress of his little brother John, who was moved close to tears at having, yet again, been ignored in the largess of his family.

But whatever the reason, she was looking at a grinning, contemptuous lad and could almost see the poisons circulating through his mind. And this young man, this Prince, this future King, was destined to become her Lord and Master, her husband, the rock on which she would build her life.

She sighed for the lot of women like her.

Part the THIRD

In which old King Henry employs all his matchless talents for war and kingship and overcomes the treasonous machinations of his wife and children and in which he looks with tender eyes upon the Princess Alys.

———— ◆ ————

Chinon Castle Touraine, in the middle lands of France on the banks of the river Vienne, June 1175

If Henry listened carefully, especially in the quiet dead of the night when the noises of the town and the castle were stilled, he could swear that he heard the pitiful wailing of his wife. Through the casements in his apartments in the Castle, the warm summer breeze carried more than the sounds of insects; above their chirps and clicks, he was certain that he could hear the sounds of a woman weeping. Sometimes, when he was in bed, lying awake and thinking through the strategies of the following days and weeks, he imagined that he could actually hear the doleful cries and desperate pleadings of his Queen, Eleanor.

Of course, it was nothing more than wishful thinking. Any wife and daughter, perhaps, any women held captive, any woman in fear of her life; any woman other than Eleanor of Aquitaine, his traitorous Queen. For Eleanor would never, ever, degrade herself by crying, by begging, by beseeching, or by being anything other than self-righteous.

She was far too angry for tears. In all the time they'd been married, and especially since he'd incarcerated her in a distant castle keep, Henry had never once seen her cry, and even doubted whether she was capable of such a human frailty as salty tears. Was she the only woman alive who was without tears?

Was it Eleanor's plaintive wail which had wakened him during the dark of the night? No! It was other ghosts and spectres which had disturbed his sleep. Even if it was possible to hear the voice of his Queen emanating through the castle's rock walls and stone floors from her tower in the far eastern part of the castle, and far away from his bedroom apartments, the only sounds she ever made were those of fury, not regret. So the things which woke him couldn't be the sounds of crying or pleading. Not from his Eleanor. She would be standing on the tower keep, between the archer's posts, screaming her demands for justice to all the world, shouting for vengeance, and demanding that the Archangel Gabriel descend from Heaven and smite Henry through the heart with His Sword of Retribution.

Yet while one part of his mind was distressed for his Queen, remembering their passion and love in the early years of their marriage, nobody, not other monarchs of distant lands, nor his Earls nor Barons, nor the entire panoply of his own Lords Temporal or Spiritual, could say that he was ill-advised in his actions of locking the bitch up. Queen Eleanor had fomented rebellion against the God-ordained King of England; she had committed treason against the person of the Monarch; she had roused his sons to rise up and rebel against him. And they had. It had taken a year to quell their rebellions. Many had died, but his sons were now cowed, beaten, defeated, bested. And all had come skulking back when he'd nearly starved them to death to teach them a lesson. All his sons, bar young Prince John who had fled France when he'd learned of their schemes, in part because of his fear of his father's rage, and in part because if his brothers were successful, then he would continue to be without a land to rule.

And all bar young Alys, who had remained with Queen Eleanor while the schemes were being hatched but decided to assist young Prince John in his return to England. It had been a hard decision for her; she didn't want to abandon Eleanor, yet she couldn't allow John, a young lad not yet in his teens, to travel across France and England alone, with no money and not resources. Knowing what was in his mind after the schemes had been espoused, Alys had left a long and explanatory note for Eleanor, swearing before God that she would not reveal a word of their plans, but she was fearful for John's life and so she was abandoning Richard to assist John to get back to his father.

The young woman took him and four guards in the witching hours of one morning, and rode north from Chinon to the coast, where she paid that morning a handsome price for a crew to sail their boat to Southampton. Then they purchased fresh horses and rode like the wind to Windsor, where they were greeted in surprise, but gratitude, by old Henry.

John immediately told his father what his mother

and brothers were planning, and when Henry looked quizzically at Alys and asked for her confirmation, she told him that she'd sworn an oath of silence, as had John, and would say nothing, ever. Understanding her plight, Henry kissed her on the forehead, thanked her for her service, and together they remained in the palace until the war between father and sons began.

The plots which Eleanor had dreamed up didn't surprise old Henry. He knew, of course, that a scheme was afoot to overthrow him, and had already gathered his forces to oppose any mercenary army which his sons would cobble together. And that is what happened.

In that way, he was able to confront young King Henry when they met before they went to war; when his oldest son and co-regent demanded England, Normandy and Anjou for himself. His oldest son was surprised when he informed him that an army stood ready to answer his demands. The young king threatened to raise his own loyal English army, but the following day, fear gripped his mind, and instead he turned around and fled to Paris and sought refuge in the Court of King Louis.

While there, the young man regained some sort of spine, and King Louis helped him draw together an army. At that moment, old King Henry was in danger of rebellion in all of his territories, all led by his sons, and one by one, though it took time and effort and many dead, he was able to put them all to rout. Each and every one of them. The old lion had stood atop the crest of a hill, looking over the landscape of his successes, and roared his defiance.

The alliance which Queen Eleanor had tried to build of her sons and those Noblemen loyal to her, collapsed against the military genius and tactical skills of old King Henry. It had taken a year of battles to put down the rebellions in all of his provinces, but he'd finally brought peace back to his lands.

And when Eleanor realised that her grand alliance, her schemes and plans, were all in disarray, she fled and took refuge with her old Uncle at Rouen. Henry attacked his Castle, but Eleanor escaped by dressing as a nobleman and fled to Paris. But before she reached the city, she was intercepted by old Henry's knights, handed over to him, and since then, she'd been locked up in the most distant of Chinon's keeps. From time to time, Henry would walk in the grounds, and look up to the top of her tower; and she would be there, standing like a bowman, looking down on him. They would talk about the warmth of the day, or how beautiful the river looked that morning;

anything but what was truly pressing on her mind. It was as though they were still a young and loving couple, exchanging the pleasantries of the day. And when he walked out of sight, he would hear her screams of anger and frustration. What a woman!

He closed his eyes, and imagined her pacing the floors of her apartments in the lofty tower, wandering from room to room like a caged lion. From time to time, he'd walk through the castle to the tower where she was held captive in her apartments in order to ensure that Eleanor was given the respect and comforts due to a woman of her stature, the daughter and the wife of kings.

Only from time to time was she allowed out into the castle grounds under heavily armed guard to wander around of the beautiful building and its lands, to sit on grassy hillocks in the pleasant, scented air, and look out over the River Vienne towards the River Loire. He even allowed her to eat some meals with him, on the condition that she remained silent and never, ever, spoke of her or their sons' treason. She'd once broken his command and tried to plead for the restoration in his favour of their son, Richard; but the conversation infuriated him and he'd ordered his servants to return her to her keep, to bind her and carry her if necessary. Her fury at the insult to her person was so great that it had taken five strong men to restrain her and actually carry her up to the tower.

But his time in Chinon was coming to an end. He would have to return soon to England, perhaps in a week, in order that he be seen in villages, towns and cities, as Monarch and King. Such progresses were necessary to people to understand why they were taxed, and where their money was spent.

In his absence from England while fighting against his sons, the borderlands of Wales and Scotland were becoming restive. Only his physical presence, to be seen atop a colossal warhorse in blinding kingly armour holding aloft a mighty sword which would cleave an enemy in two, would quell any discussions of rebellion. If these nations of Scotland and Wales which owed him allegiance, which paid him tribute to prevent his army swarming over their borders, suddenly seceded, it would be a problem. For then he'd have to raise a larger army, which meant more taxes would have to be raised from the barons, which would have to come from their peasants … and that mean starvation for the people, which would lead to further quarrels with his Barons and Earls.

Of his many children, legitimate and illegitimate, only his legitimate sons were the real bastards, he would tell his courtiers. Not only did they fight against each other, but they were now fighting him for possession of land. But he'd defeated them all, and fined them so heavily, that they'd had to beg for food like the poor and diseased outside inns and alms houses. But it was an important lesson in choosing which enemy to engage, in which battle to fight, how to marshal an army to best effect, and most especially, at what point was your enemy sufficiently unprepared or weakened, that an assault would succeed.

And then there was the question of how he could dispose of Eleanor. The danger of her being in Chinon, apart from the disruption she caused to the castle and even the village, was that she was within two week's march for an army coming from Paris, and while the French King would never dare to try to conquer Henry's lands, he was able to use the excuse that he was merely attacking the Castle to release Queen Eleanor. Perhaps the French king could hear her screams of denunciations and threats made to heaven, all the way to Paris. It was certain that many of the people in the village below the castle could hear the madwoman screaming from her tower, and there was always the danger that what she was saying could get back to the French king. So she couldn't remain here in his castle at Chinon, but would have to return to England with him.

Which led his mind to the question of where she would be imprisoned. In Sarum Castle in Wiltshire? Or perhaps Winchester Castle in Hampshire? Either would be capable of restraining her, and she would be well away from the Noblemen and women who may still have felt some sympathy for her as Queen, if not for her causes as leader of a rebellion.

These days, Henry rarely slept a complete night. This evening, he'd been awake to see the sun rise over the River Vienne, and the first movements of the peasants in the village below the walls of Chinon Castle. He swung his legs from under the covers, pushed aside the curtains which surrounded his bed, stood, and walked to the table stand where fresh water and a chamber pot had been left for his ablutions.

Refreshed and emptied, he slipped off his nightcap, his nightgown, and stood naked before the chamber window in the warm early morning summer air, breathing in the delicate scent of tulips, daffodils and lilies, as well as the more pungent aroma of crops bursting with seed like wheat, maize and barley. If he could live his life like this, as the owner of a simple castle with a village below his walls to provide him with food and livestock, dues and offerings, without wars and disputations, without having to administer justice and internecine battles for supremacy with his own children...if he didn't have a wife who would see him spliced in two with a battle axe if his back was turned ... if he didn't have Earls and Barons vying for preferment and judging his every move to see how it benefited them ... if only he had all these things, he would be a happy man.

But that wasn't the lot of a king, and especially a king of England and Aquitaine, two of the most desirable and wealthy domains under the realm of God. The lot of such a king as he was first to gain the throne, and then to spend the entirety of his life defending his ownership against avaricious nobles and princes, wives and brothers, and every jealous fellow monarch from over the borders.

Not for Henry the luxury of spending more than a catch of breath in thinking about anything other than the protection of his realms. And today, that defence would continue, for once he'd put on his loincloth, longhose and braies, he'd call for his servants to finish dressing the upper part of his body. They might still be asleep on the straw outside of his chamber, but once he opened the door and called for them, some occasional cold mornings requiring an additional kick in their bellies, they'd spring up and attend to their lord's requirements.

A short time after waking, Henry was sufficiently well dressed to descend into the banquet hall, where the kitchen staff had already laid out his breakfast of chunks of freshly cooked bread, slices of meats and fish, anchovies, slices of fruits, and jugs of ale and wine. It was too early for his nobles and their ladies to rise and join him, and so he contented to break the night's fast on his own.

Until a young woman entered the Hall, and his life. He noticed the movement immediately, and looked at who was walking into his presence. Tall, full of the grace of a noblewoman, with long blond hair and with a shining morning face which was both beautiful and full of promise, Henry was both startled and delighted. More so when she emerged from the shadows into the Hall and he saw that it was the young Princess Alys who had unexpectedly entered into the Banqueting Hall. She came from the direction of her apartments, and was equally as surprised to see the King, as he was to see her.

"Lady Alys. A pleasure. So early," he said.

"My Lord King. I wasn't expecting…if I'm disturbing… I'm so sorry … I'll return to my rooms …"

"Please, Princess, come sit with me and share my meal.

Why are you not asleep at this hour? You're not unwell, I pray," he said.

She walked over and sat opposite him. "No, indeed, your Majesty. I'm very well. I rose early with the intention of riding. I love to ride through the woodlands and fields in the early hours of a summer morning. It fills my heart and my soul with God's delight."

The moment she sat down, a servant took plates and knives from the buffetiere, and set them before her.

King Henry pushed over the platters of food and said to the servant, "And bring over one of those new instruments so that the Princess can stab the food and not dirty her fingers. As for me, I've used my fingers all my life, and truly can't see the value of these things, but you're young and elegant and you're about to go out riding."

She thanked the King for his generosity and thoughtfulness, and then proceeded to skewer food onto her plate, knowing that with the exhilaration of the ride, she'd be ravenous by mid-morning. What she didn't realise was that the king was looking at the grace and delicacy of her every move. Nor had he noticed over the years that she'd developed from child to woman and become tall and willowy, slender and restrained, more a delicate branch of a flowering fruit tree than a cavorting child.

Since his quarrel with Richard, and the growing distance and hatred between sons and father, he was thinking of sending Alys back to King Louis, even though he knew he'd have to return her dowry and that it would severely hamper trade and commerce between the two nations, and that meant that the King's revenue would diminish. He was still thinking that she should marry Richard, yet since his treason against the Crown, since he had clearly sided with his brother young King Henry, and with Geoffrey, then an alliance between Princess Alys and his traitorous son Richard, joined by those nobles loyal to Eleanor, would no longer be acceptable.

So to avoid sending her back and losing her dowry, to whom could he marry her? King Louis VII of France would only accept another Prince in the stead of Richard, and especially one who might become King. If not young King Henry, who had been married at the age of three for the past fifteen years to Margaret, another daughter of Louis and his second wife, and she'd brought him good land in her dowry, then as Richard and Geoffrey were traitors, the only legitimate son left worthy of the hand of a Princess, was Prince John.

But John was such a sallow, pallid, mewley, weak little boy, driven by childish desires and emotions, that the idea of him ever attracting a woman other than a whore, a courtesan, a trull and a strumpet, was difficult to conceive. Of course, he'd entertain an arranged marriage, but no daughter of worth will willingly give herself to such a supine *impuissant* as he would no doubt grow up to become. God help John if ever he was to acquire a Kingdom, for the Earls and Barons would force him to his snivelling knees to do their bidding, within hours of his coronation.

Henry shuddered at the thought. And then he looked over again at the delicate young woman, fifteen years of age, ripe and youthful, yet wise beyond her years; dutiful, polite, yet – when Eleanor was calm and talkative, had described the young woman as wilful, determined and headstrong. A force to be reckoned with, a match for any real man.

Give her to John? Henry smiled. The boy was half her age, and even when he acquired manhood, he'd never be man enough for a woman such as Princess Alys. A woman like her would need a stallion to ride her, a Solomon to equal her wisdom, and a Caesar to command her.

It was then that Henry realised that he'd been so busy

with his family squabbles, with his fury with Eleanor, with the fractious state of his lands in open revolt as they sided with his sons, and with his wars and battles, that he'd barely had time to notice Alys. And although he'd seen her first when she was only eight, in the years since, she'd grown into a beautiful girl. Almost a woman. Not a woman like Rosamund, of course, but a girl who would soon become extraordinary. In some ways, she reminded Henry of Eleanor when she'd first come to him after she'd been annulled by her husband. She had been then a woman of thirty, but of extraordinary beauty, mature in face and manner, sylphlike as a nymph and delicate as the finest cloth voile. She was reputed to be the most beautiful woman in the world, and when he first saw her, even when he was just a nineteen-year-old and bedding every wench who walked past him, she took his breath away.

But that was Eleanor, still handsome but of a poisonous nature. And now that he truly looked at Alys, he saw that she was growing into the same depth of beauty, yet there was a calmness, a gentleness, which was never part of his feisty wife's composition.

But give Alys to his son Prince John? It was too silly a thought to contemplate. Nor was she for treacherous Richard or Geoffrey. So who?

And then a thought occurred to him which surprised him, until he received yet another unexpected message from his groin. And to his astonishment, he realised that his groin was continuing to send him messages about Alys. So early in the morning? And the more he looked at the young Princess, a virgin of a girl, gracefully sipping her wine and eating her fruits, the sharper and more insistent the message became.

It wasn't until later in the afternoon, after he'd attended to matters of state, and begun uttering directions to his seneschals to begin the process of quitting Chinon Castle in order to remove the Court to England, nor until most of his Lords and Ladies had retired to their apartments to rest or dress for the evening's banquet, that he was alone in the Hall, and able to think about the affairs of the morning.

While he was breaking his evening fast, his mind wandered to the early morning's appearance of Alys, so he was distracted when the Princess suddenly appeared again, intending to find food in the Hall. She had deliberately missed the luncheon, as she did every day, because now that her Queen protector, Eleanor, was incarcerated, she preferred to visit her and eat her meals in that company. Henry had found out through his servants that the Princess felt that she was alone in the Court, that she had no supporters or friends, and that it was like being in enemy territory.

So her visits to the Queen had been willingly granted by Henry, not wanting to be cruel to Eleanor, but now also knowing that Alys, was alone and bereft, separated from her mother protector and estranged from her treasonous finance Richard. The child was in a state not unlike the Church's *limbus patrum*, the Limbo of the Fathers, where she was in the friendship of the powerless queen, but not yet accepted into the grace of the powerful king. Yet because none of these events were of her making, Henry had taken pity on her and allowed her freedom of movement and even the right to keep company with his traitorous queen.

When he saw her enter the Banqueting Hall, he called over for her to sit with him.

"But Majesty, I was simply here to find some food and retire to my apartments. I don't want to disturb your Majesty's presence," she told him.

"My work is done, Princess, my orders given, my court has retired to their rooms in order to prepare for the evening's feast, and I am alone with my thoughts. I would welcome the distraction of a young and beautiful woman."

Dutifully, she walked over to the table, and sat beside him. The King turned to her, and said, "My Princess, because of the distraction of this past year while I have been putting down rebellions, I have paid less and less attention to my Court. It has come to my notice that you feel abandoned, like a frail leaf adrift on a mighty river. If that is the case, then be assured that your interests are central to my heart. Not for a moment would I want you to distress yourself about your role in this Court, about the place you have in our hearts as our dear beloved daughter, nor about the disposition which will fall to you because of the treachery of your husband-to-be Richard."

"Thank you, Your Majesty. But since the imprisonment of your Queen, my heart has been heavy, both because of the treachery you have suffered, and because of the actions of Her Majesty and your sons," she said softly, fearful that she might say a word or a phrase which could implicate herself in the eyes of the King.

"Which brings me to a matter weighing on my mind. Since, Princess Alys, you cannot now contemplate marriage to my son Richard, it is incumbent on me, both *de jure* and *de facto,* that a suitable husband has to be found for you. I have been thinking of my only loyal son, John, but …"

She looked at King Henry in utter horror, her face displaying her immediate feelings. "Majesty ... you cannot ... John!"

"But now that you are a woman of fifteen summers, eight of which have been spent here in my Court, and John is but a boy of nine summers, you will be a matron of twenty by the time his manhood is properly equipped to enter you. Yet if I don't marry you to him, then who is to be for you? Apart from Richard, who is *persona non grata* in my heart, there is only Geoffrey, who has come to me and begged my forgiveness, which I have willingly given. But he has been promised to Constance of Brittany since she was a babe. If I disrupt the wedding plans and take him away from her, then I will have to fight and win yet another war. So I intend for them to marry in a few years' time.

"The son of one of my Earls might be man enough to bed you, but his title and station of birth cannot equate to yours as Princess daughter of the King of France. The insult to your father and family would be too great and I will have to fight yet another battle. As things stand, there is nobody of the rank of Prince in my court who is able to offer you the status in marriage which is your right by birth," he said.

She nodded. "These matters have been pressing on my thoughts since Richard and your other sons, other than John of course, turned against you in such a way. As you know, Majesty, I was in Chinon when the decisions of rising against you were being taken, and though I tried to speak reason and counsel against it, your son Richard told me that I have no voice in family or courtly matters, because I am merely a woman."

Henry burst out laughing. "Like Eleanor is little more than a woman, yet she came within a hen's beak of overthrowing me; like Lady de Claire or Baroness Gloucester have no voice, yet somehow both speak their opinions so loudly that my ears can't hear what I'm thinking."

Alys burst out laughing. Rarely was King Henry funny when he was surrounded by his Court; but when he was surrounded only by his family, or his mistress Rosamund, he was at times delightful. As he was being now.

She hesitated to say the words, but they were an unspoken presence between them. "Then, Majesty, send me back. Return me to my father and my family in France. I'm still young enough for a suitable match in another kingdom, and ..."

Henry waved his hand dismissively. "Impossible.

Your dowry has become a crucial part of my lands. I enjoy much revenue, and trade, from those lands which were your inheritance, and which passed to me by your contract of marriage. No, Alys, the cost of returning you would be simply too great to bear. So here you will stay.

"But you cannot remain here without the prospect of a husband. And my sons Henry, Richard and Geoffrey are both unworthy of you, and unavailable. John, we both agree, will not be ready for a woman until you are too old for him – though I was a lad of nineteen and Eleanor was thirty when we wed, and for months on end, she rode me all night and all morning until I was barely able to walk – but John is not his father; he is no old King Henry, I regret to say. Which ..." He let the rest of his thought rise into the air.

Alys looked at him in interest. "Which? Your Majesty? You have a suggestion," she asked.

He looked at her, then sat back and gazed at the distant ceiling, then looked at her again ... and then burst out laughing.

"Sire? Henry? What are your thoughts. It concerns me, and so I beg you to speak."

"Which ... discounting my four sons by Eleanor, and as my other sons who are illegitimate and would not be acceptable to your father Louis, leaves only one man who could become available to you … if circumstances changed."

Then Henry looked down at the table, and picked up morsels of his food, slipping them into his mouth, waiting to see whether Alys, a very bright girl, would pick up the trail of his thoughts.

It took her just a moment for her face to change from ingenue to that of a woman horrified, before she said, "But Queen Eleanor. Your Queen. You're still married to her. Under God. Till death do you part … Unless." Then she crossed herself, twice. "Oh dear God, no! You cannot think of executing Queen Eleanor, like Herod the Great executed his Queen Mariamne … It cannot be, Majesty. Yes, Eleanor committed treason, but she is one of the most admired women in all …"

"Execute Eleanor!" he shouted, and then burst out laughing. "God forbid. Dismiss and banish that thought immediately. Execute that woman? And have ten armies descend on England seeking my head? NO! Heaven forfend … though God in heaven knows that she deserves it for her treason, for her conspiring with my sons, for fomenting them to rise against me, to enlist armies and try to depose me … yes, for that I could, and could behead her ten times over, for that's how many crowns she wants to wear.

"But for a woman like Eleanor, the only course forward is for me to divorce her. Despite our many children, the Pope would grant dispensation for a divorce, especially if I increase the Annates I pay him this year. Then I would be free to marry, and if you agree to become my wife, you would be Queen of England and my lands in France. Not just the wife of a Prince as you would have been in marriage to Richard, but wife of a King, an English King; a queen in your own right. Queen Alys of England and Aquitaine. How would your father Louis enjoy that status for his daughter? Then you would no longer be just his daughter, but his equal."

Too stunned to speak, Princess Alys opened her mouth, but closed it when no sound came out. She wanted to laugh or cry, but was still too shocked by his offer. Yet how could she? How could she participate in the destruction of the only mother she'd ever known? How could she sit back and witness the humiliation of Queen Eleanor? By becoming the instrument of her own downfall and imprisonment, Alys couldn't … wouldn't … add further to the woman's distressed circumstances and misery by marrying the man she truly loved with all her heart.

"Majesty, Henry, my Lord King, I'm flattered beyond measure, but I am your ward. The contract you signed with my father Louis. And the difference in our age ... the hurt that would inflict on my mother Eleanor ... the ... no, Majesty. It can't be contemplated," she said, her face towards the table, too frightened of the King's reaction to her refusal.

Henry nodded as her objections ran their race and she was again left speechless. Softly, he said, "When I was playing out the possible plans in my mind, Princess Alys, I too laughed when I came to my name. Yes, you are my ward. And yes, I'm older than you, but that means that your marriage to me will be short, and on my death, you will be Queen Dowager ..."

"As will Queen Eleanor," Alys said. "On your death, you will have two former Queens, and God help me as the younger Queen when the old Queen turns her anger towards me, as most surely she will."

"True, and that is an issue with which you will have to contend. But fear not, child, for Eleanor won't be your enemy, not when she's still my prisoner, even long after my death. I don't see Eleanor warranting her freedom, during my life or when I die. In confinement, she is just a bird of prey shrieking into the sky. But free of confinement, she will gather an army to herself to inflict a revenge against me which equates with the battle of Armageddon fought in the heavens above. The rocks and cliffs of England will ring for evermore to the sound of her fury. So Eleanor will stay in her confinement until the day of her death, be she my wife, my widow, or be she divorced from me." Henry took a draft from his goblet of wine, and looked at Alys.

Hesitantly, Alys said, "Forgive me Majesty, but when you die, another king will take your place. Young Henry. And he will ensure that his mother goes free. And that means that my life will be in danger."

"Alys, these are turbulent times. We are all at risk; even me, a great King. My sons rebel against me; my wife foments rebellion; by barons and earls and knights are restive and would happily stab me in the back if it were to their advantage. We, who sit upon the highest seats in the land, are all in danger. We keep two eyes on the path in front of us, and one eye behind. You will be surrounded by loyal guards, well paid upon my death; they will protect you. But," he continued, "coming back to the matter of marriage to me. Yes, Madam, I understand your reluctance. Marriage to an old warhorse like me cannot be as appealing as marriage to a young buck fresh in the saddle. So let me propose a potential solution. As you know, my mistress, the Lady Rosamund, is unwell. She has not come with me to France, but has retired to her home in Wales to recuperate. We all pray that the malady which ails her disappears and that she recovers. I've sent two of my physicians, the Jew Abraham of Mainz and the Frenchman Rene Joseph of Reims, to England in order to attend to her. Reports say that while she is still weak and vaporous, the air of Wales seems to be beneficial for her. I pray that within the next months, she will recover and return to me.

"But her illness leaves me in bed alone at night. Yes, I could have any of the Ladies of the Court, but none moves my manhood, and it would cause much bad blood with the noblemen to whom they're wed. So my suggestion to you, and at this stage, Princess Alys, is that it is a suggestion and not a command, is that you come to my chambers tonight in order to attend to my body's needs. I shall leave the banquet before the riotous assembly begins its skirmishes. And you, Princess Alys, will have the honour of sitting beside me at the banquet tonight," he said.

She felt her face flush deep crimson. "My Lord ... I ... but if I sit beside you, the entire Court will be lively this night and for the weeks to come with talk about me, that the King has taken his ward as his new mistress. In no time, the whispers will fill Queen Eleanor's ears, and how long before somebody tells my dearest friend, Rosamund in Wales what I have been forced to do. I will be ruined …"

"Nonsense, girl. Being the King's mistress is one of the greatest honours which can be bestowed on a woman by the Crown. I will not force you, Alys, but if you refuse me this simple gift, then your value to me will diminish, and I can see no reason for your continued stay in my Court. When, next week, my court returns to England, why would you continue to be a part of us? What reason, Lady, would there to be for you to remain. You won't, of course, return to France and your family, so perhaps a year in the cold and barren north of my lands, a castle on the borders of Scotland, may persuade you better of the warmth you will enjoy with me in London or Windsor or even Woodstock, than any honied words from my kingly lips?"

And to old King Henry's surprise, Princess Alys merely stared at him, without speaking, opened her mouth once or twice as her flushed cheeks suddenly drained into a ghostly white, and she slithered from her chair to lie beneath the table in a dead faint.

Part the FOURTH

In which old King Henry takes Princess Alys away from his courts of Aquitaine and Windsor, where there are too many ears and eyes, and settles her into his newly refurbished lodge, Woodstock in Oxfordshire, which he had expanded for his mistress, Rosamund.

Woodstock Lodge river Glyme, in the county of Oxford, a day and a half ride north-east of London, August 1175

Well ahead of his company of fifty lancers riding as guardsmen, whose horses carefully negotiated the forest's trees and its muddy paths leading towards his favourite hunting lodge, Woodstock, the Princess Alys rode beside old King Henry on her charger and wondered what precisely the King held in store for her when they arrived.

She raised herself in the saddle hoping to look between the trees of the forests through which they were riding. But as they rode forward and mounted a hillock, and when she raised herself in the saddle, she was still unable to see the Palace he'd described to her in such loving detail. The forests were so dense that she could barely see the sky through the canopy above their heads.

"Close by now," the King shouted, short of breath due to the exhaustion of the past two days' ride. "Not more than a matter of a few leagues. When we breast the next hill, you will see my lodge in the distance. Then my guards will ride to Woodstock and establish the household there, but I will settle you in a group of buildings which I have had constructed nearby. They're very comfortable, and there will be no other persons there, other than your maids, your Ladies if you so desire them, and guards posted throughout the night outside of your doors. If you wish for just your maids, then your Ladies can stay in the main Palace. Oh, and my Princess, a drawbridge connects your dwellings to the main building so we can wander freely in and out, but once the drawbridge is raised, then where you reside will be separate and private from the rest of the world."

Princess Alys shouted, "Thank you, your Majesty,"

and continued to ride beside him. But she knew, because she'd been told so by one of her maids, that the lodgings of Everswell, where she and her small entourage would be housed while they were at Woodstock Palace, had been built specially for the accommodation of the Rose of the World, the Fair Rosamund, the King's mistress, Rosamund Clifford, who was lying ill and prostrate in Wales, praying every day to recover in order to return to the King's bed.

Princess Alys felt hideously uncomfortable filling Rosamund's bed, her apartments, and her designated role as the King's Mistress, which she knew she would become tonight. Alys loved Rosamund, just as she was loved by her. And she knew with absolute certainty that if, or when, Rosamund heard that Alys was about to become the King's mistress, almost certainly while in her own and special apartments at Woodstock, the dear, sweet, loving woman would understand her predicament, immediately forgive her, and wish her well.

But though she knew that she must become the King's mistress or suffer banishment to the cold and inhospitable wilds of the North of England, she was also excited about seeing the wonders of Everswell. It was reputed to have a spring and a fountain, as well as three interconnecting pools in which she could bathe unobserved for her modesty, yet at the same time, be more free in her body than she'd been since she was a babe.

As though he understood what was going through her mind, the King said, "My masons were sent by me to the Southern parts of Spain, where there is a Moorish Palace called Alhambra. I wanted them to see how to divert a stream so that it flowed to a fountain near one of my Halls, in order that spouts of water could be seen dancing in the air. The Moors, though godless, know how to do these things. My men spent many weeks there, they didn't understand what they were told, and so they brought over two Moorish builders, and it was they who constructed what you will see."

Despite the effort of talking and riding, Alys said, "That sounds beautiful, your Majesty."

"Yes. I saw it last time I was here, in Woodstock, and it was truly amazing. You know, my grandfather, King Henry, the first to take that name for the English throne, turned these buildings here into a hunting lodge. The vast amount of land enclosed within the walls Henry built contain some of the best hunting in all England. In those days, he kept deer and boar and hogs and rabbit, of course, as well as lions and leopards as a special sport.

The animals from Africa are all gone now. Poachers, probably, despite my gamekeepers roaming the grounds at all hours of day and night. They've found the bones of some of the poachers, who were probably taken by the last of the lions. Vengeance, indeed.

"And I improved the buildings and made the living areas more luxurious so that Rosamund and I could spend many days of leisure here. Just as I hope that you and I will spend days, now that I'm installing you in the Everswell houses," he said.

They rode side by side and as they reached the top of a hill, in the distance, they saw Woodstock, and nearby a separate series of dwellings which Princess Alys assumed was where she was being installed as the King's mistress. So Everswell would be her home, as well as the cemetery of her good name.

Though he assured her that he would be discreet and that nobody would know he'd gone to her lodgings shortly after she left the meal, and though she begged him to remember her reputation as a maiden, a Princess, the daughter of the King of France, and an unmarried woman; and though he explained how he would slip in and out of her Everswell apartment buildings without alerting his guards and her Ladies, she knew that the chances of old Henry secretly visiting her were slim.

Everything he did was on an enormous scale ... his movements, his voice, his height as he towered over underlings, the manner of demanding, rather than requesting when he spoke to anybody ... he was not a man who lived life under the cloak of any form of subtlety. Though he might truly intend to keep his visits secret, and had told her so twice, Alys knew in her heart and mind that there was no possibility of that happening.

Only the flares of burning torches, soaked in pitch between Woodstock and the drawbridge to Everswell, lit her path in the evening dark of the night. She followed the pools of light which illuminated the pathway, and soon found herself inside the main building where she was met by three women of her household, who all curtsied, and then stood to examine her. They had been recently employed from the nearby village of New Woodstock. The house's Seneschal, who had arranged their employment as dressers, maidservants and women of the privy, had told the women that it was important that they attended well upon the Princes Alys, not just for themselves and their income from employment, but also for their community. The new town was desperate for the King to grant it a Municipal Charter, which would add to its status and income from travellers, allow the townspeople to petition the local Bishop to build a church, and change their status from serfs to burghers. Now that she was to become the great King's mistress, she would have influence on his thoughts and mind, and so it was in their interests to treat her like a queen, and not a young whore pleasuring the King of England.

As she walked into the Hall, the oldest of the three women, Katherine, who was designated Maidservant, walked over to her, and said, "Welcome to Everswell, Your Highness. I'm Kate and this is Meg, who is your Lady of your Privy, and this is Anne, your dresser. How can we be of service to your Majesty? Do you require a change of dress in preparation for the arrival tonight of His Majesty, the King? We've changed the straw in your bed chamber which is now fresh and flavoured with the scent of rose and apple blossom. We've rid the bed of bugs and made it clean and fresh. We're told by the Seneschal that his Majesty greatly appreciates those scents. But he didn't know about your desires. Is there a scent which pleases you?"

Suddenly shocked – yet part of her was not surprised – Alys gasped, "The King? His Majesty? Who informed you that the King will be attending me here?"

Kate suddenly flushed in embarrassment. "Oh! Highness! I didn't mean ... the Seneschal told us that ... but ... Oh! By the blood of Holy Christ Jesus, I'm sorry. I didn't mean ..."

The old woman looked horrified by her error. "How can I make amends? Highness, I beg of you not to blame Meg and Anne for my error. Dismiss me, but not them. They need this work ... my mouth is always getting me into ..."

"Stop!" insisted Aly. "Woman! Stop! I'm not angry with you, or the other women. What you said just surprised me. I didn't expect you to mention the King's person. I am here because ... he is not my ... His Majesty, the King ... but I ..."

And then she drifted into silence. What was the point of trying to keep this matter private between herself and the King. It would be the talk of the land in days and weeks to come. So either she should admit her imminent downfall, or she should resign herself to a year spent in the cold, dark corridors of a northern English castle.

She took a deep breath, and looked at Kate, then Meg, and then at the last of the women, Anne. For the time she was here, these three women, unless she dismissed them, would be with her in these rooms almost every moment of her time. They would dress her, clean her, ensure her hair and jewellery were properly done for her meetings with the King. And inevitably, because they would be the only people with whom Alys would talk to beyond the King and his small entourage, she knew that she would say intimate things which they would keep to themselves. Indeed, it was known that servants who spoke of their master's and mistress's secrets beyond the bed chamber had sometimes been put to prison or even executed. Yet although they were strangers, with no mother, no sisters and no Rosamund, these were the only people in whom she could confer.

"Well," said Alys, "as you will be my maids and no doubt will observe those who come in here and those who leave, and on the condition that no word of this is spread by any of you beyond these walls, then you may as well know that His Majesty King Henry will visit me. He will make me his own in the bed where he and the Lady Rosamund used to ... where they ..."

"Lady Princess," said Kate, "we're all grown women here. We know what His Majesty the King does in these rooms."

"But not with me!" Alys insisted. "Not until now. This will be my first ... I am a maid still. Innocent. A virgin. Unbroken. Until tonight when he comes to visit me. And in Christ's Holy truth, I'm sorely afraid of what he will do to me."

She knew that as a Princess, she should have held her counsel, but she was so frightened and alone, that her heart suddenly burst with the need to tell somebody ... even her maids ... what was terrifying her.

But suddenly Kate, old enough to be her mother, seemed to melt like snow in Spring, and she said, "Oh, my poor child. There comes a time in every lass's life when she opens her legs to a man and becomes a woman. And bless you, Princess, but Meg, Anne and I have each and all of us known half the men in this country. Some because we wanted, some because of the debts of our husbands, and some because we were taken by force.

"I became a woman when I was but a child of twelve years. A visiting scholar told my father that he'd teach me to read for just a penny. He took me by the banks of the river. Taught me no words, though. He just took me."

Then Anne interrupted, "Just as I was taken by the blacksmith when my father couldn't afford to pay for repairs to our kitchen pots. We couldn't eat, and so my father gave me as the price for fixing them. He took me beside the forge. It hurt, but it was warm."

"And I," said Meg. "I lost my innocence to my oldest brother. I was but a child of nine when he took me. He told me it was ordained by God, and that Eve was Adam's sister, but I told my father, and he beat my brother half to death."

"Your Highness," said Kate, "every woman in the village has a similar story. Every woman, as a young girl, was taken by some townsperson or over-master, or, in many cases, by a brother or father or uncle. What's going to happen to you has happened to every woman here, and throughout England. It's the lot of a woman to be taken by men, and our lot, since the time of Eve, is to lie there and accept our fate. Just because you're highborn and the daughter of a King, and soon to be the mistress of a King, doesn't mean that his Majesty will be doing anything different to you than what my husband does to me every night, when he's not too drunk. Or Meg's husband. Or Anne's."

Alys sat on a chair and looked at the three women. They could all have been her mothers or her older sisters, and their look was one of empathy, a consoling and understanding sharing of the sisterhood into which they'd all been born. Regardless of birth, rank, position or title, they were all women whose God-given purpose since the time of Adam was to bear the fruits of their loins, to nurture their babes, and to provide satisfaction to their men's desires.

She nodded, and asked quietly, "Then how can I prepare myself for His Majesty's visit? My mother died when I was a babe-in-arms, and I have only had the Lady Rosamund as my guide into adult life. Yet never did we talk about these issues. In court, our discussions were about things not of the body. So I sit here bereft of what is expected of me tonight. I've prayed to God and the Virgin Mary, but no answer has been forthcoming.

"Am I expected to perform? Like a dance or some act which will please His Majesty? Am I dressed for his first greeting, or do I appear naked? How do I touch His Majesty? What pleases a man? There is so much to know, and I have no knowledge of what is to be expected of me," she said plaintively. "Shall I ... am I supposed to ..."

The three older women looked at her, then at each other, and suddenly knew precisely what to do. Kate and Meg had done it for their daughters before they married, and Anne, though her children were too young yet, had been told in precise terms by her mother what her husband would expect of their wedding night. And although the Princess Alys was the high-born daughter of a King of

France and they were merely peasant women from the local village, they were all women under the gaze of the Almighty, and as such were sisters in need.

So they walked forward to where Alys was sitting, knelt before the Princess, and softly, gently, but in vividly descriptive terms, explained precisely the role that she should play when the King came over the drawbridge of Woodstock, and entered Everswell.

And come, he did. King Henry the Second, by the Grace of God King of England and Aquitaine and lands beyond the Sea, was already merrily drunk as he tried to enter Princess Alys's apartments. Yet though he feigned treading on tiptoe across the drawbridge so as not to disturb the household, he entered Everswell's hall when the two guards opened the front door, but the noise of his taking off his sword and placing it on the banqueting table, would have woken the dead.

As advised by her maidservants, the Hall was in semi-darkness, scented with the erotic essences of sandalwood, lavender and rosewater, which Alys knew to be the King's favourite perfumes. Despite the gloom, illumined by candles in the corners, even in his drunken state, Henry could see his way past the table and furniture to a lighted corridor which he knew led to Rosamund's bed chambers, where Alys would be waiting. Although he collided with a large dining chair which tipped over under his drunken weight and clattered on the floor, he corrected himself, and wove his way into the corridor. At the end lay her bed chamber, lit by a pathway of candles on the floor.

"Oh Alys," he whispered. "Sweet my Alys!"

"Here, my King," she said. Her voice, quivering because of her nerves, was higher pitched than normal. With her maidservants, she'd spent much of the later part of the afternoon practicing what she would say and how she would appear when the King first made himself known to her. She'd prayed to God that he would appear alone, and not with a Seneschal, or the head of his Guard, or some other man friend who had come to see her downfall. Any such observance would dramatically increase her concern of public exposure and destroy her reputation even more quickly. Yet when King Henry first appeared alone on the threshold of her bed chamber, he stood almost as high as the door's stone lintel, weaving slightly, and obviously trying to focus his eyes on where Alys stood within the room.

And the effect which her maidservants had spent hours perfecting appeared to have succeeded. Henry looked at her in amazement. She was standing, deliberately positioned in front of ten candles which cast their piercing light through the flimsy voile garments she was intentionally wearing, so that the outline of her tall, lean, youthful, fresh and delicious body was clearly visible through the cloud-like fabric. Though he couldn't see details of her private woman's parts, her breasts and the delicate and now-perfumed bush below, the King's piercing gaze and opened mouth showed that his mind was rapidly drowning in lascivious thoughts.

"I ... Jesus, Mary and Joseph ... you ... Princess ... I had no idea. You're beautiful. You're a woman. I didn't ... I came ... I didn't come here ... expect ... Your Grace, help the King remove his clothes, so that I can make you my own," he muttered, walking unsteadily towards the bed. He pivoted and fell backwards onto it, holding his legs in the air so that she could remove his boots, stockings and then reach up and remove his braies.

Although she'd been instructed what to do when his undertrews were removed, she had told her maids that, no matter what, she wouldn't use her mouth, regardless of the King's demands or the potential repercussions of her refusal. They had explained in great detail what pleasure it gave a man, but the idea of that ... thing ... in her mouth ... disgusted her.

Instead, Anne, who was just a dozen years older than Alys, told her she, too, rarely used her mouth when satisfying her husband, but had developed clever ways of blocking his view with her body and using her hands, well-oiled with warm liquid goose fat, and pretending to moan in pleasure, to the same effect. So skilful was she that her husband never knew the difference between hands and mouth but derived enormous pleasure from it. So much pleasure in fact, that often he would reach completion without her need to receive him inside her body.

Her maidservants had taken some goose fat from the kitchen and melted it in a dish held in place over a candle and sweetened it with essence of lavender so that the smell of burning animal fat wouldn't be detected.

Anne told the Princess that of a weekend, when she and her husband were alone in their room, she would pretend to use her mouth, and he was in such ecstasy with the movements of her hand, that he never once demanded access to her body, which came as a great relief.

And now, bereft of her maids, she was alone with the King and all responsibility was on her shoulders to ensure his happiness. She'd laughed and joked with her maids, but as of this moment, her life was held in her own hands, and at the whim of the King, it could go from heaven to hell.

Finally, she pulled down the King's undergarments, exposing his nudity. But now that he was naked from his waist to his feet she was able to observe at close quarters the reality of her situation. She looked at his Royal Member and was so horrified that she felt sick. Unlike what had been described in graphic detail by her servants, and their descriptions had been amusing and colourful, it wasn't at all what she'd been anticipating. Henry's member was red and gnarled and wrinkled like a month-old piece of meat, covered by white hairs, with blood-red veins dark and prominent on the surface. Yet she knew she had to close her eyes and her mind to the obscenity of what was expected of her, and so she dipped her fingers into the bowl of warm liquid goose fat, grasped the King's manhood, and proceeded from there.

King Henry suddenly opened his eyes, both in shock and at the unbridled joys of the warmth and tender coaxing he was experiencing. He looked down to see what she was doing but her body was positioned in such a way as to block his view. So he looked up at the back of Princess Alys head with an admiration bordering on hunger. Roused by her gentle subtle hands, the King reached up and pulled her down onto him, hugging her and kissing her neck, cheeks, and lips. And as she'd been urged by her maidservants, she climbed on top of him, raised her chemise and straddled the lands of both England and Aquitaine.

And as instructed by her wise and all-knowing maidservants, Alys closed both her mind and her eyes to the pain she suddenly experienced, and to what the King was doing to her. Instead of concentrating on what was happening inside her body at that moment, Alys instead thought of herself alone in the warmth of the French countryside, running up a hill until she reached the top, then standing in the warmth of the summer breeze and viewing the landscape below her. She started to count the imaginary houses in the nearby village, the spires on the churches, the distant castles. And she continued counting the buildings, rocking backwards and forwards by pivoting on the King's person, suddenly her Royal lover beneath her moaned, shuddered, gasped and cried out aloud. He continued shuddering and crying out, concerning Alys that he was in the throes of dying. And then he stopped, and his body suddenly seemed to empty itself of its vitality. He breathed out deeply, as though sound asleep, yet his eyes were open, and he was staring at her in an almost trance-like state.

She had been told by her maidservants that the cries and moans and yells were the expressions of a man when he had finished and emptied himself, and so she waited until his last shudder before rolling off his body. Then she quickly went to the basin of warm perfumed water which had been left by her servants. There she took a cloth flannel, squeezed it, and returned to the King, wiping his manhood. He continued to lie there, looking up with unseeing eyes into the canopy of the bed, whispering things which she could barely hear.

Alys returned to the basin, where she washed away the blood which was still flowing from her fractured maidenhead. From beneath the bed, she quietly slipped out a bowl of liquid filled with a concoction of fermented apple cider, vinegar and aloes of foxglove which had been made by Anne and Meg that afternoon. She'd been told by her maids that if she invoked the name of the Virgin Mary three times with her eyes closed and her left hand held over her heart, and then silently rubbed the brew over and into the lips of her womanhood, it would prevent a future pregnancy.

She did as she'd been instructed, listening carefully to the King's gentle breathing to ensure he didn't see what she was doing below the level of the bed. Then, when the witch's brew had been rubbed in, Alys cupped water in her hand to force a draught of cooling liquid into her womanly passage to wash out the king's deposit. Then she inserted a clean cloth inside her to catch the flow of blood before standing, straightening her shift, and returning to the bed to sit beside the King. She had done everything which her maids had advised, and to their enormous credit, it seemed to have worked. Certainly, she would reward them all the following morning.

"Is your Majesty satisfied? Did I behave as you had hoped I would?" she asked softly.

He looked across to her, and softly asked, "Swear to me that you were a virgin before tonight, Alys. Swear it on the sanctity of the mother of Jesus."

"I swear, Your Majesty," she said.

He shook his head. "I know you're telling the truth, Princess, but I still can't believe it. Your hands are more skilful than a mason's, your lips more subtle than a two penny whore ... and your womanhood ... as young and tight and passionate and beauteous as anything I've enjoyed. Yet I am your first man? Tell me again that it's true."

"Majesty, you've broken my maidenhead, my

coverage. I am bleeding. That alone tells you the truth. I swear by all that's holy that you are the first man who has ever known me," she said, trying not to show her emotions.

"But how are you so ... how did you know what to ..." he asked, still amazed. "I expected to have to teach you. I thought you'd just lie there and ..."

For the first time that afternoon, indeed for many days since Henry had made his claim on her, she smiled and then laughed. "If I tell you, Majesty, I pray that you won't be angry and punish me."

"Of course not ..."

"This afternoon, while you were with your guards drinking and feasting, I came to my chambers here in order to prepare for the evening. I was nervous, as it was to be my first time with a man. I was about to lose my innocence and I didn't want to disappoint you. My maids, those women from the village whom your Seneschal chose to serve me, were waiting. And when they saw my concerns and knew that I had had no mother since my birth, they advised me of what a King would expect of his mistress. And I followed their advice," she said. She looked at Henry to see his reaction, hoping that he wouldn't be annoyed.

But instead, he looked into her eyes, and then he burst into laughter. Coughing and spluttering, he managed to gasp, "I shall make these servants into the highest nobility of the Court, for they have been of greater use to me by their action than all the wives of my Earls and Barons and Lords put together. Tell them, sweet Alys, that they will be well rewarded for their service to their King." And he continued to laugh until he slipped off his doublet and his under-vestments and lay naked. Then she gathered his nightgown from beneath his pillow, slipped it over his head and shoulders and straightened it. Exhausted from the drink and food, and now from his loving embrace and coupling with Alys, he struggled off the bed to stand on wavering legs, took a chamber pot from beneath the bed and pissed into it. Alys covered it with its cloth, while Henry rolled himself over onto the side of the bed, slipped beneath the covers, and within minutes was asleep and snoring.

And Alys, now a woman and the King's mistress, straightened her chemise, slipped her slender body beneath the covers on her side of the bed, and tried to restrain the pictures playing in her mind so that she, too, could drift off to sleep.

Everything appeared to have changed when she and

the King crossed the drawbridge from her apartments in Everswell, and entered the banqueting hall of Woodstock. Since waking early, being dressed by their servants and going to Chapel to pray, both King Henry and his mistress Alys were hungry and ready for the meal to begin their day.

Food had been prepared for breaking their fast, and as they walked in together, servants bowed and hurried to place platters, knives and the new pronged instruments onto the table in anticipation for the arrival of the food. One servant cleared the side table for the arrival of the breads, pottage, boiled meats, rabbit, partridge, peas and beans.

But it wasn't the food, or the servants preparing for their Majesties to eat, which had changed. The difference between this morning and the previous mornings when she was in the Palace of Windsor or the Palace Tower in Westminster, was that in those palaces, she was barely noticed and rarely acknowledged. Now, as she walked beside the King, her arm threaded through his, she sensed a distinct transformation. Guards who never even glanced at her when she passed, made a point of bowing their heads in deference as she walked before them in the company of the King; servants who may have smiled at her because she was a young girl suddenly were bowing and curtseying as though she were a senior member of the Royal family. Even the Seneschal of Woodstock, one of the most important people of the household, bowed low to the King as he entered, but quite deliberately bowed low and deferentially to the Princess. The King failed to notice the difference in attitude of his servants, but Alys did, and was amused by it.

Henry and his mistress sat down at the table, and dishes and cutlery were immediately placed before them. Starving after a night of sexual fun and a deep and relaxing sleep, followed by an hour of Chapel, Henry picked up slices of meats, bread and spooned pottage onto his plate, which he began to devour immediately. Alys used her prongs to stab a few slices of rabbit and partridge, picked up a lump of still-warm bread, and sipped some ale from her beaker.

It was the first time that Alys had officially eaten in public with the King. She'd shared his table a number of times in the past weeks, but only when she happened to be passing him while he sat at a table and he invited her to sit; not at a prescribed meal time where the court was formally in attendance. Something about her situation told her that this was a special moment in her young life.

And her feeling was confirmed when she looked around the room and saw that six or more servants were standing around the walls of the banqueting hall, waiting for a glance or a wave of the King's hand at which point they would hasten forward and do his bidding.

But what she noticed most especially was that the servants' eyes were on both His Majesty, and on herself. No longer was she a curiosity or an adornment or even an addition to the Royal entourage, there merely by birth or position. Now, she was part of the Royal family, an attachment to the King, integral to his Majesty's life, a person in her own right; one to be observed, respected and attended.

Somewhat mischievously, she decided to test her new potency within the King's hierarchy. She looked up and caught the eye of the Seneschal. Then she arched her eyebrows, and waited.

The man immediately left his position by the nearby wall, walked over to the table, and asked, "May I assist, your Majesty?"

"Yes, I'd like some cheese," she said.

The Seneschal bowed and said, "Immediately, Majesty." Then he turned and clicked his fingers, which caused two servants who'd overheard the request to scurry to the kitchen. Moments later, a platter carrying a large roundel of cheese as well as slices was brought out and placed before her. The King didn't even look up from his meal, yet despite herself, it was such a new experience that she could barely restrain herself from smiling. No longer was she a child of the court, tolerated because of her future as wife of the son of the King; no longer was she ignored as she walked into a room where people glanced at her and discounted her because she was of no immediate importance; and no longer was she seen as a burden on the tolerance of the Royal family.

Now, although a whore in the eyes of the court, she would become a woman of status, of stature, simply because she was attached in body and heart to the King of England. Apart from the Queen, no woman had greater status in the echelons of the Royal family, than she. All she had had to do to climb the ladder of social hierarchy from her place near to the bottom, to her place beside the King, was to open her legs, close her eyes and accept the Royal benefaction.

Was her sacrifice so great? Was the gift of her virginity to the King so boundless that her life had ended in her bed the previous night? Looking around the Banqueting Hall at the deference she was being shown by the servants, the answer insisting itself upon her mind was clearly no! But Alys was a girl who thought both of the present and of the future, and for the moment, revelling in her newly endowed status, she was content to put the future where it should be.

After their meal, the King excused himself, telling her that he had state business to attend with a gentleman of the court, who had recently arrived that morning. He suggested that Alys return to her lodgings in Everswell to prepare herself for some hunting in the afternoon. They stood, and she curtsied deeply and respectfully, to show the servants that while she may be the King's mistress, she knew her place in the order of precedence. But to her unutterable joy, the King gently lifted her up by the chin, and said for all to hear, "Princess Alys; this is now your residence. While I remain the King, you, Madam, are queen of Woodstock and Everswell."

Then he turned to address all the servants and the Seneschal who were watching. "And let that be known throughout this household; that the Princess Alys is a special favourite of the King of England and speaks on his behalf while in Woodstock."

The King then kissed her hand, bowed to her, and retreated down a corridor towards the library where he would greet the gentleman of the court who had recently arrived, and conduct the business of the nation.

For her part, she retreated to her rooms. As though floating on a cloud of happiness, Alys walked alone from the Banqueting Hall, over the drawbridge, and into her chambers in Everswell. There she was greeted by her three maidservants, Meg, Kate and Anne.

Unable to restrain themselves, now that she was alone with them, they all forgot about precedent and their places in her service and crowded around her, as though she was their best friend.

"Well," demanded Anne. "What happened? Was it as we said it would be? Was the King happy? Did it hurt? How much did you …"

"Silence, girl," said Kate. "Her Highness can only answer one question at a time. Well, Princess? How did you fare last night?"

"It was as you said," Alys told them. "I followed your advice and performed precisely as you told me I should. I washed my womanly body in the vinegar and aloe mixture, cleansed myself of His Majesty's deposit, then …"

"Yes, yes," interrupted Meg, "that's afterwards. But the beginning, Princess, what happened when first you began

... when the King first ... as he walked in ... when he ..."

"At first," said Alys, "as you told me, I stood only in my shift before the candles and allowed their light to show him my body through the fabric. That deeply affected him. Then it was all of a moment. Suddenly, he was on the bed and I was helping him to undress. And when I removed His Majesty's under-trews ... when I saw ... I hadn't expected. I was shocked when I saw his ... it wasn't like you said it would be. It looked more like old sheep meat kept hanging for too long. So I closed my eyes and let my hands give him pleasure. Then, as you all advised, I ... well, you know what I did. And His Majesty seemed very pleased. Oh, and I told him who had advised me to act in that way, as I have no mother and relied on women of experience to tell me what to do."

Suddenly horrified, Kate felt faint when she heard the words. "You told His Majesty. About us? What we advised. Oh Jesus, Mary and Joseph. Was he ... did he ...?"

"Kate. He burst out laughing. He was amused. And he was pleased that I had been wise enough to seek counsel, and that you had been forthright enough to have told me what was expected of me. His Majesty said that you three maidservants were of greater value to him than all the wives of all the noblemen in the country, and that he would reward you. Don't be so afraid, all of you. King Henry is fierce and noble, but he is also a good and loving man," she said. "I shall remind him of your service to me, to us, and ensure that he rewards you well for your counsel."

Yet Kate, as well as Meg, was worried that the King had become privy to their private and intimate conversations about him, and everybody in England knew that his mood could turn on a penny piece. If he felt that his privacy was now a public matter, then all three women could lose their heads, no matter how sweetly young Princess Alys might behave towards him. Yet she was either oblivious to the danger posed to them, or they misunderstood how different was the King towards this young Princess than to other courtiers. It was known that he had been a different person when he in the past he had stayed in Woodstock with the Lady Rosamund, and that he'd been milder and kindlier towards his servants and members of the nobility. But they were risking their necks with this young woman, and their fate was now a matter of whether the Princess Alys truly knew her King, or whether she was assuming that his courtesy towards her also meant the same for her staff.

"Now, His Majesty wants to go riding and hunting when he's finished the business of the nation. Meg, Kate, please set out my hunting clothes. Anne, fill a pitcher of fresh water from the well so that I can refresh my mouth and face after the food," she ordered.

They hurried off to do their mistress' bidding and in moments, Alys re-entered her bed chamber where her riding and hunting clothes had been assembled on the bed for her to assess. She nodded and smiled, stood in the middle of the floor with her arms raised, and Meg and Kate walked towards her to remove her morning clothes. Standing only in her under-garments when Anne walked in with a fresh pitcher of water in a ewer, she washed her face, swilled water around her mouth, and dried herself with a towel. It took just moments for the maidservants to dress her in her riding clothes, put on her long boots, and then arrange her hair so that it was tied down against the effects of the wind. The King was known to be a very fast horseman and few could keep up with him. He would probably canter beside the Princess, until he spotted a deer or a boar, and then the spirit of the hunt would overtake him, and he would suddenly scream out a blood-curdling curse, take an arrow from his quiver, fit it into his bow, and ride at a breakneck speed towards the fleeing animal.

Only God knew whether the young woman would be able to keep abreast of him when he was in full gallop. It had been known that the Lady Rosamund gave up trying to keep apace with the King when she had been his lover, deferring to his vastly greater skills as a rider, soldier, and man of action. But there was so much about this young woman, Alys, which was unknown, that nobody was willing to guess whether she would keep pace with her lover, the King of England and Aquitaine.

Part the FIFTH

In which the Princess Alys establishes herself as a firm favourite in the heart of King Henry II, much to the concern of the court in general, and the imprisoned Queen Eleanor in particular.

—•—

The White Tower, in the city of London two months later October, 1175.

She wondered whether her days of bliss were at an end forever. Whether the unutterable joy she'd experienced for the first time in her life was just a dream, or whether it had really happened. For weeks, the Princess Alys had been respected, even admired, by the servants of the King and the courtiers who came to Woodstock to pray for the King's attention; for weeks, her days hadn't been full of hurtful remarks from the King's sons or denigration couched in politeness from senior men and women of the Court.

And most especially, for the months of August and September, warm and sun-filled months with balmy nights and the gentle scent-filled air wafted through casements in zephyr breezes, she had laid in her lover's arms at cockcrow in the morning, made passionate love to him in the night, ridden and hunted with him in the day and made love again in the afternoons. Then, while he was dealing with affairs of the nation, she spent the early evenings dressing to please him and the small court which had gathered to be close to his presence. While he was old enough to be her grandfather, Henry was besotted by her, enamoured of her, captivated by her and infatuated with her body. It was as though every time he touched her, Alys's youthfulness seemed somehow to flow from her body to his, and for the time they were coupling, he was like a young buck, rampant and robust beyond his years. Even in the short weeks since he had made her his own, the King's drinking and cavorting with his men-friends had diminished, and when he attended her in her chambers, he was not just clean and sweet-smelling and amorous, but wise, funny, kind and gentle.

Each and every night, seamstresses somehow created

one new gown or item of clothing for her to wear to please the King, in colours which would have made a rainbow jealous. And it wasn't just the joy of her bed chamber which changed her life. Once the word spread that King Henry was in Woodstock with his new mistress, troubadours, jongleurs, peripatetic players and minstrels entertained them and their court every night, each performer going away with a purse of money and the gratitude of the King and his Lady.

Once a week, when the King was restless, he and the Princess Alys would ride with their escort of bowmen and lancers over the hills and through the valleys of Oxfordshire to pay an unannounced visit to the nearby family of one of the noblemen and women of England. Delighted to be visited by His Majesty and thrilled by the surprise, the noble family always welcomed and treated the King and his Lady to a sumptuous luncheon or dinner before they rode back to arrive in Woodstock as the sun was setting. Alys wondered whether the King knew that his Seneschal, who learned of the King's planned visit for the following day, speedily sent a guardsman to forewarn the hapless family.

But as the days grew shorter with the onset Autumn, the King's business became more and more pressing, and one evening he said to Alys, "I have to return to London. We leave tomorrow morning. Matters need to be attended and my presence is essential. You will return with me. We shall stay in the Tower of London, which will suit us both well. The castle is very comfortable, and you will enjoy the grounds and the banks of the River Thames. In attendance will be officials of my court, as well as my advisors, but most of my court will remain in Windsor."

And so, without seeking any approvals from her for the sudden relocation, Henry and Alys rose in the morning, breakfasted and rode south and east towards London Town in front of their mounted bodyguards. Before she left, she thanked her maidservants. Already well rewarded for their many services, Alys ensured that she gave each a sizeable purse as her way of thanking them. When Meg, Kate and Anne looked inside each of their purses, they gasped and cried aloud. Just from the weight alone, it was the better part of a year's income for each of them.

Late in that afternoon, as the company thundered along the pathway which ran beside the north bank of the River Thames, they breasted a hill, and there before them was the Tower of London. Tall, bold and standing like a pillar against the dark, muddy slow-moving water of the river, one look at White Tower failed to give Alys any comfort. It immediately struck her as the finger of God standing tall in defiance of the river. The tower, its surrounding buildings and walls stood out starkly against the many crude mud and wattle buildings on the northern shore of the river. Smoke rose through the straw of their roofs and dissipated into the air, leaving the surroundings of the Tower cloaked in what looked like a noxious fog.

Some of the nearby buildings were built of wood and in the distance, she could see blacksmiths and woodworkers, shingle makers, tanners and weavers plying their trade in the surrounds of their buildings. It was so different in aspect from what she had grown to know and love in Woodstock, where the trades were hidden from her and carried out in the local village, but her home there was surrounded by fields of crops and fruits.

As she looked, she compared it in her mind to the delights of where she had just spent the past many weeks, to Woodstock and Everswell, charming buildings set in the lush and uplifting greens and yellows and reds of the English countryside. The air of Woodstock was always scented with the fields of flowers and leaves of the trees, and was a delight to breathe. But since they'd been riding along the banks of the Thames, the stench of decay and death, of rotting meats, dead bodies and putrid earth, filled her head with disconsolate thoughts.

She glanced over to the King, and saw that he was smiling when he viewed one of his favourite residences. He looked towards her, and shouted over the thunder of the horses' hooves, "Magnificent, isn't it. It was built by my grandsire, William of Normandy when he crossed the sea in order to conquer the Angles and Saxons of this land. They lived in mud houses and had never seen a building such as this. He built it to show the strength of his army, to warn them that rising up against him was useless, and that he and his followers were now the rulers of England.

"And by God, did it work. It's told that people came from far and wide just to view the height and magnificence of the Tower. And he put it to good purpose, both in the dungeons below as prison for traitors and miscreants, and as a residence for himself and his family.

"Look over there, dearest Alys. See the moat and the two defensive walls which circle the Tower. Not even the armies of the Roman Emperor Augustus could have breached that defensive position," the King said.

"It's a wonderful building, Your Majesty," she shouted back, and continued to ride abreast of him along the muddy path of the pestilential river. She tried to put her dark thoughts behind her as they rode nearer and nearer to the Tower, but no matter how she tried to block out the thoughts, the charm and freshness of Woodstock kept impinging on her mind.

Without a mother, Alys didn't know who to ask. Without her maidservants, Kate, Meg and Anne from Everswell, she had nobody with whom she could confer. Only the King's physician could answer her questions, and his Majesty was so busy with matters of State that she didn't want to bother him.

Yet ... yet she had to know. Her womanly flows had begun when she was twelve, and she was used to them. They came every month, usually on the fifth day of the month and lasted heavily for a matter of two days, during which she remained in her room; then the flows diminished and she was able to attend the court in Windsor Castle, to eat and drink with the company and to behave normally.

And she had anticipated their arrival on the fifth of October. But to her surprise, and relief, no flow came from within her body. Nor did it appear on the following days. And to compound her surprise, she was suffering an ache in the small of her back. Her maidservant, a surly and unwelcoming older woman called Liza, from the local area, fetched her a warm cloth to relieve the discomfort, but it only worked as long as the cloth retained its heat. Alys badly missed her friends Kate, Meg and Anne from Woodstock, for they would have helped her understand the changes which she was now experiencing and their cause. She considered sending for them, but in the end, Alys decided to beg the King's pardon, she asked if she could be attended by his physician.

Because of his sudden involvement in those matters of State with which he had to deal, the King spent most of his time away from Alys and with his courtiers and counsellors. They slept and dined together, but his mind was so distracted by the nefarious activities of his wife and sons, of the Earls and Barons of his Court, of the disputations along the borders of his realms, of England's relationship with the Kings of France, Spain, Portugal, not to mention the Holy See in Rome, that he and Alys rarely spoke in loving terms. Even his love-making was peremptory, little more than a relief for his body from the stresses of the day. In Everswell, he had been a lion, teaching her much about the joys of the body. But in the Tower of London, he was more of a man who needed her support than her lover.

Yet as they were walking from their bed chamber to the dining hall, she asked him whether she could see his physician, Isaac the Jew.

"My physician … are you sick, my Lady? What's the matter?" he asked in concern.

"No, Henry. I'm well. But I have this ache in my back and I want to know the cause and the cure."

Later that morning, there was a respectful tap on the doors of her chamber. Liza walked over and opened it.

Isaac the Jew, wearing his physician's cloak and cap, white-bearded, bent, but with kindly eyes, stood there, and said, "His Majesty has ordered me to attend upon the Princess Alys."

Princess Alys stood, and welcomed him in. "Liza, give our distinguished guest a cup of mead," she ordered. Her maidservant reluctantly poured one from the ewer, and took it to the physician, who by this time had sat down before the Princess.

"As an old man, I need my few comforts, Highness, and mead is one of these few. Now, may we talk openly, or would you rather we were in private?" he asked, nodding towards Liza.

"Leave us," Alys ordered. Her maidservant shrugged, gathered up the small tapestry she had been threading, and retreated to an antechamber. When the door was firmly closed, Isaac asked, "His Majesty tells me that you have an ache in your back."

"Yes, it's been here for some weeks, and it won't disappear. I've sipped a concoction of the hollowleek and bishopswort, but they provide no relief. It doesn't affect me greatly, but ..."

"And tell me, Highness, has your monthly flow ceased?"

Surprised that he would know this, she answered, "Yes. I was expecting the flow in early October, but it failed to arrive. It's now some two weeks overdue, and ..."

The old man smiled. "Highness, I could beg your indulgence and ask you to lie on the bed while I examine your womanly parts, but there is no need. It's obvious what ails you ... what is your condition. This is no illness or ailment, Highness. You are carrying the King's child. You have a baby growing in your body. A gift of the Almighty God. A royal baby, whose birth can be expected in ..." he thought for a moment before saying, " ... July of the coming year. A summer baby, full of light and love and happiness."

Alys looked at the old man. Her jaw sagged. And

then his words impinged themselves on her mind, and it all became so obvious. She'd seen younger women of the court suddenly disappear for months while they undertook their confinement and later lie-in.

Isaac could see the shock on the young woman's face. She reminded him of his granddaughter, a beautiful girl who had wanted to follow in his path as a healer, but had been disappointed when told that all she could ever aspire to be was a midwife or woman who made medicines from herbs.

"Highness, you seem shocked. Forgive me. I assumed that you were familiar with your body and its fluxes. May I be allowed to explain what will happen over the next many months?" he asked softly.

The Princess nodded, and Isaac continued, "Women of your rank, Highness, normally realise they are with child after only three or four months of pregnancy, despite their body trying to inform them. As a physician, I'm privileged to give this diagnosis early in a woman's term because of my experience as a physician. In a few months, when the baby begins to grow and the effects are seen by the swell of your stomach, then custom demands that you take to your chamber for your confinement and remain there until a month after the birth.

"Windows will be closed and tapestries hung over them to reduce the light which comes into the room. Only one window will remain uncovered, and it may be opened, depending on the effluxions from the river. These tapestries will be carefully chosen to be calming and gentle, so that you and the babe will see only the joy of God and His angels.

"Only women may attend you. No men, not even His Majesty, will be permitted to enter your confinement, though having been His Majesty's physician for the past many years, I don't know of any man, woman or beast who would be able to prevent the King from attending upon you.

"Being a devotee of the Catholic faith, your ladies in waiting will bring you crucifixes and prayer books which will be placed on your naked stomach, so that the babe will be as close to the Lord God as is possible. In that way, God, your Jesus and his mother, Mary will look upon the child with grace and favour. Some midwives favour amulets or even amber to lie on the mother's stomach in order to assist in the birth.

"The reason your room will be darkened, is to recreate the conditions of the womb, dark and silent and warm and comforting, with no outside noises and influences to frighten the child. My view is different, Highness, but I won't be there and so I won't contaminate your mind with my thoughts. Because now, Highness, we come to the moment of birth in the middle of this coming year. A pregnancy lasts for nine months. You have been pregnant, I would assume, for one or two of those months. I will not be attending you for your confinement. I am not allowed, being a man, unless the King orders it ... and I would hope that you can prevail upon His Majesty because of my experience in delivering babies.

"But if I am forbidden, then you will be well-attended by midwives who are greatly experienced in the art of giving birth. They will do things to your room which I find silly and unrewarding, but as I won't be there, be comforted by the fact that these women have great experience in the delivery of a healthy babe.

"Now, the question which will be filling your mind. Will you feel pain? Yes, great pain, but it will last for just a short time. God has ordained this pain in childbirth as punishment against all women for the sins of Eve and the expulsion from the Garden of Eden. Her original sin of seducing Adam with the fruit of the Tree of Knowledge, has meant that women such as you ... all women throughout the ages ... must suffer great pain without relief of medicine. Only the assistance of prayer and holding your crucifix, will offer you any comfort. It's also said by some midwives that clutching pieces of cheese or butter with prayers inscribed on them, brings relief, but I have always doubted such nostrums. It is also said that prayers to Saint Margaret will assist you. She was the saint who was eaten by a dragon, but it spat her out when it realised that it had also ingested a crucifix along with the woman. Saint Margaret is the patron saint of pregnant woman, so praying to her will do no harm. Women pray that the birth of the child will be as painless as the way in which Margaret slipped out of the mouth of the dragon.

"The midwives which I will supply are well chosen, both for their experience and their honesty. Some evil and unscrupulous midwives, especially those who attend the poorer classes, secrete on their persons and out of the bed chamber, the birth cord and its blood, and the placenta which joined the baby to the mother, in order to sell them to witches who use them for evil purposes. But my midwives are scrupulous in taking nothing whatever from the birth chamber. And they will dictate the best position for Your Highness in which to give birth, whether it is in birthing stool, or on the bed on your knees and they will take the child from behind, or perhaps two of the women will cradle Your Highness as you lie in their arms while a third midwife helps the babe escape from your body.

"But I stress, Highness, that while you will experience great pain, this unfortunate condition will last only until the arrival of the babe, and once its head emerges and the midwives twist its tiny body so that its shoulders slip out of you, then all pain immediately disappears and you're free to revel and delight in the mystery of giving us yet another Royal babe."

He sat back and sipped his mead, while he waited for his words to be absorbed by this lovely child, this naïve adolescent woman who more and more reminded him of his beloved young granddaughter.

At last, Alys spoke, "Master Isaac. I was born and my mother died within days of my birth from the fevers of childbirth. All my life, I have been in the company of boys and men; rarely have I enjoyed the company of women. Only one, the Lady Rosamund who was like an older sister to me.

"So I have never been told of what my body does, nor of womanhood, nor of childbirth. I thank you, Master, for being patient and explaining what I will suffer. It brings me comfort, for knowing and not fearing is the way of overcoming alarm … and believe me, until your arrival, I felt little but alarm," she told him.

He fought back a smile, trying not to think of this tender young woman as anything other than the mistress of the king, and not as a young girl, like his granddaughter. Yet how could such a young innocent, such a beautiful and ingenuous child, be the lover of an old man like King Henry? Even such a thought, if it became known, could see him thrown into the dungeons.

Yet how could he think otherwise. Having seven children and two grandchildren who had been raised by the tenets of the Jewish law, where love of God was the same as love of family, it was incomprehensible to him. Yet he had observed so much outrageous, immoral and ungodly behaviour among the men and women of the court, that for his own safety, despite his position as physician to the King, he closed his eyes to what the lords and ladies of the court were doing.

As a young physician, he had travelled to Baghdad and studied the writings of the great Shabbethai Donnolo, the Italian Jewish mystic and doctor, and there he had met with many other physicians who taught him much. More recently, a young man in Cordoba in Spain by the name of Maimonodes had attracted him because of the depth of thought he brought to his work as a physician. But the one thing each and every one had strongly advised him was not to become emotionally involved with his patients. Rather, to treat each one dispassionately as though they were little more than bodies to be ministered, bandaged, splinted and treated with herbs and nostrums.

Yet how could he, as a grandfather, father, husband, Jew, physician and human being, a student of the Jewish law, of the wisdom of the elders, and a beneficiary of the love of the Almighty God Yahweh, God of Abraham, Isaac and Jacob, not look at this pathetic, bereft little girl and not feel his heart pouring out to her. She was so young, so delicate, so vulnerable and innocent. Like a leaf in a storm, she had been battered by forces so powerful that she was in danger of being crushed. And as his heart felt as though it was melting under her ingenuous gaze, he determined that in place of her dead mother, her distant and uncaring father and any who could give her love and comfort, he, Isaac the Jew, would be the rock upon which she could now brace her young body against the crashing waves he knew were gathering.

It wasn't until later that evening, long after the banquet had finished, the entertainers had quit the Tower of London, and the Court had retired that they could be alone.

She didn't know how to raise the issue with Henry, who was exhausted and close to sleep as he walked into their bed chamber. But by good fortune, a memory suddenly impinged itself on his mind, and he asked, "My physician, Isaac the Jew. Did he attend you? I ordered him to."

"He did, Henry," she said, as he fell back onto the bed so that she could remove his boots and garments. "And he gave me information which …"

Though close to sleep, he opened his eyes, and asked, "… which?"

"Which informs me that you are to be the father of my child in the middle of next year. I hope that pleases your Majesty," she said, almost in a whisper.

"A child? A child!" Suddenly the sluggish monarch was animated and sat up on the bed. "A child? My child? My son? Dear God in Heaven, why didn't you tell me earlier? This calls for a celebration. I'm to be a father. With you. My young and beautiful Alys. God be praised. I shall order a special Orison to be sung tomorrow. *Lucis Largitur Splendide. Thou bounteous giver of the light. All glorious in whose light serene.* That was written by your countryman, Bishop Hilary of Poitiers, you know.

"Oh joyous Alys. This is splendid news. You've made

me so happy. But the name? What shall we call him? Robert? Thomas? Walter? Do you have a preferences, my Lady? He can't be Stephen, of course. My first son, Henry, died, and I won't name him Richard or Geoffrey or John who have acted so cruelly against me. I could call him William, after the conqueror of these lands. Yes, that's a good name. William! We shall call our son William."

"And if our child is a girl, Henry?" she asked tentatively.

He remained silent, and just looked at her in love and devotion. "If a girl, then we shall find her a suitable husband, and she shall be queen of a land beyond the seas. France, perhaps if Louis is deposed and another monarch takes his place who isn't close in blood to you. Spain? Portugal? Somewhere warm and sunny to suit the disposition of her mother."

"Yet if our child is a boy, Henry, will you allow him to live within the palace, or place him, like others of your bastards, in the home of a courtier? Because if you are considering such a move, my Lord, then I must beg you to …". she began, distress creeping into her voice. But because she was becoming emotional, she found she couldn't continue.

"Madam," King Henry said softly, "you are worrying

yourself over matters which have yet to come to pass. My long life informs me that the only things of true concern are the things which are about or happening at that moment. I am the King of England. Supreme monarch and overlord of all. I decide which of my family stays and which leaves, which is favoured and which diminished, which is raised up and which is dashed upon the sharp rocks of circumstance below. Be assured, Lady, that our son will be favoured because he is the outcome of our love, not the unwanted product of a whore I happen to have favoured one drunken night."

"And Richard? Geoffrey? John?" she asked.

"Those miscreants … they raised their arms against their father, and their hands contained weapons dedicated to my death. And more than their fists, for they also raised armies and I had to put them down. Many of their men died as a result of my sons' greed and avarice. But do not include my son John as one of their number. It was Prince John who returned to England to warn me of their plot. He, and he alone of all my children, including my son Henry, was the only one to remain loyal to his King, his father, and his family. As to the others, now that they have been defeated, now that they are bereft and expunged from my good graces, they are trying make amends. And know this, sweet Alys. I will forgive them. That may shock you, for you aren't a monarch. But they are the heirs to my kingdoms. By birth, by right of succession, by primogenitor, Henry, Richard, Geoffrey and even John will inherit my lands ... when I am dead. But John is a boy, not yet able to rule. One day, he will become a great king, but that day is some time off. So now that I am an old grey beard and my time is limited by God to three score years and ten, only the Almighty knows if I will have the strength to still be king when our son, yours and mine, is old enough to take up sword and lance and ride though our lands, proudly proclaiming that he is the right Royal son of a king," Henry said.

She was going to respond, but Henry's eyes were already heavy and due to close any moment. So soothingly, she helped him lie down on the bed, kissed his forehead, and despite being fully clothed above the waist, pulled the blankets and downs over his body. By the time she'd arranged them to ensure they didn't cover his face, he was already asleep and beginning to snore. But if the King gave the appearance of sleep, his mind was a cookpot of new ideas as a result of Alys's amazing news.

King Louis VII of France had been married both to Eleanor and subsequently to Constance, women who had only produced girl babies. But, he thought, what if King Louis can't produce a male offspring? If that becomes the case, then what of the throne of France? It would be, and remain, vacant until given to the husband of one of the daughters of Louis. And Alys was his daughter. But that meant an annulment of his marriage to Eleanor, which would cause untold problems with some of the Kings of that place, and especially with the Pope in Rome. Yet Eleanor had tried to overthrow, and probably hoped for the death of her husband so that her sons could inherit his lands and realms. He had once hoped that one of his sons, Henry or Richard, married one of Louis' daughters such as Marguerite and Alys, could and should become the King of France. But since his children had risen against him, and since he was now about to have a new son with a woman totally unlike Eleanor, a young woman who was totally loyal, demure, uncontesting, mild and gentle, then why shouldn't he, Henry of England and Aquitaine, also become King of France? And with that thought, he smiled, and drifted off to sleep.

Seeing her lover smile, Alys drew back, and looked at the father of her future son. And as she saw his grey beard and the diminishing red of his once-flaming hair, now almost completely white, she wondered whether he would be alive for her son's birth; and if so, whether she could persuade him to disinherit his treasonous sons, including John, annul his marriage to Eleanor, and marry herself, the woman he truly loved above all others. Not that she was being a silly girl for thinking so, because the King had spoken of his love for her and his plans for their future together.

And if she could somehow succeed in her grand disposition, put away his present family and his wife, then she, Alys, Princess of France and soon-to-be mother of the male child of a king, would become Queen of England and Aquitaine, and her son ... William ... would eventually become King of England ... and Aquitaine.

Old Sarum Castle, Wiltshire, close to Salisbury ... a month later, November 1175.

Sitting in her private chamber beside an open mullion window despite the cold, dressed in a wrap of furs to keep herself warm, Eleanor, Queen of England and Aquitaine, now prisoner of her husband King Henry, was suddenly distracted from reading a scroll sent to her by her sister, Countess Marie of Champagne. She had been enjoying the writing enormously and was immediately irritated by the distraction. The scroll had been copied from the writings of a young man, Chrétien de Troyes, and was about some old English king called Arthur and the knights in his service who sat at a round table and went in search of the Holy Grail. His writing was so expressive, so beautifully structured and poetic, that if ever she was to regain her throne next to the King, she would invite Chrétien to England to enhance her court.

But the distraction, from some distance away and coming from the direction of town of Salisbury was a lone rider, surrounded by a small company of armed guardsmen. She tried to discern a pennant which could indicate who the rider was, but the group was still too distant.

And as she continued to watch them ride at speed towards the castle, she realised by the clothes and riding habit of the person who approached her, that it was a woman. Now, having lost the writer's argument in her mind, she put down the parchment, and continued to look at the approaching company. And as they came to a sufficient closeness that she could begin to identify them by their armour, she knew that she recognised the horsewoman in the centre of the guardsmen. It was the woman who had stolen her husband, the woman who had warmed Henry's bed for the past ten years, the woman they called Fair Rosamund because of her generosity, her kindliness, her beneficence.

Yet she was riding, alone, though guarded, into Eleanor's castle. Why? For what possible purpose? To gloat at her imprisonment? Surely not. Nobody, other than Henry's bum-lickers, would be so bold and unforgiving.

Then why? What possible purpose could fair Rosamund have for her visit, to ride north out of Wales all the way to Salisbury, two hard days pace at a gallop, and especially when reports spoke of Rosamund's sickness. It was told to Eleanor that Rosamund spent more time lying in bed ill and taking nostrums, than she did walking through the hills and valleys of her primitive land of Wales.

Curious beyond measure, Eleanor roused herself and paced down the steps to the upper courtyard gallery, where she could observe from above the gates being opened to admit the riders, and the Lady Rosamund Clifford getting off her horse.

Not long afterwards, in the freezing cold of the late November morning, she called down an order to her guards to escort the Lady Clifford into the Greeting chamber of the Castle. Eleanor also instructed that

Rosamund's guard was to be disarmed, then escorted to the heat of the kitchen, where they would be given hot food and drink to warm their blood.

Sitting in her carver before a hastily assembled feast, Eleanor looked to the entry as Rosamund walked into the Greeting chamber.

"Please, my dear, come sit by me and warm yourself before the fire. You must be freezing after a gallop on such a cold morning. Here's hot food and drink for you," Eleanor told her.

Taken aback by the Queen's generosity, and having been wary of how she would be greeted on such an occasion, Rosamund entered the chamber, and bowed low in deference to her Queen.

Amused, Eleanor said, "Such formality, Mistress Clifford. When you see me, do you see your Queen, or a prisoner of your lover, the King?"

"Majesty, you were and remain my Queen. Though your husband took me as his mistress when I was little more than a girl of sixteen, and …"

"He took you, Lady Clifford, because you were then, and remain, one of the most beautiful women of this land. Yet perhaps it's the ride which has made you look wan and drawn, or you are ailing. I've heard that you spend many days abed, taking medicines," said Eleanor.

"Majesty, I have little more time left upon this earth. It is my intention to retire for what God grants me as the rest of my life, and to take the veil in the Nunnery of Godstow. As to being the King's mistress, Your Majesty, yes, it can't be denied, and nor do I wish to go to God with falsehood on my lips, lying to my Queen, despite what I have done to you and what you have suffered as a result of me," she said, sipping some hot mead and eating a morsel of bread.

"Is that why you've ridden here to see me? To apologise? To make amends for the hurt you have caused, the insults to me as Queen and wife of the King? When I was absent in France, he flaunted you as his wife and queen before the entire court. The lords and ladies of England paid you homage. You sat beside my husband on my throne ... MY throne, madam. And I am supposed to forgive you, just because you intend to sequester yourself from your sins, to become a nun and take the veil? As you end this life on earth, you expect that God will forgive you your sins and your impertinence. Well, Madam, He might, but I'm not all-forgiving. Yes, you were a child when my husband took you, but even a child can say NO! Forgive you? If that's the reason for your journey,

Mistress Clifford, then I fear it's been a wasted ride."

"No, Majesty. That isn't why I've spent three days riding here. I'm here not for myself, but for a different reason, a different person. I'm here to beg your understanding for something which came to my ears a week hence, and of which I need both to inform you, and to ask for your understanding," she said, looking at the queen to try to determine her state of mind.

Suddenly curious, Eleanor asked, "Not for you? Then for whom?"

She took another draft of the warming and refreshing mead, and wondered how to begin. "Your Majesty, many years ago, a young girl came from France to England to engage herself and her fortune with your beloved son, Richard …"

Frowning, Eleanor sat forward in her chair, and said, "Yes … yes … young Alys. What of her?"

Taking a deep breath, Rosamund said softly, "Your husband, the King, took her when I retired to my bed in Wales. She had been his mistress since the summer."

Shocked, but trying not to show it, Eleanor thought of young Alys. Tall, thin, but attractive, yes, it was now obvious. Having been rejected by Richard, she was of little or no value to the Court, and despite Eleanor's misgivings, Eleanor needed to consider that her son, Prince John might make a suitable match for Alys. If not, the young French girl would be returned to her father, King Louis VII in Paris.

But now she was the mistress … and that would have happened when the child was only fifteen … Eleanor was of no value. And knowing old Henry, he would be loath to give back the lands he'd acquired as part of the marriage contract and would find a way to retain them.

"My husband, the King, has many mistresses, Rosamund Clifford. It surprises me that you aren't more annoyed at the Princess Alys, than you expect me to be. After all, it's not my place she's usurped, but yours," said Eleanor.

"Highness, that's only a small part of the information which came to my ears a week last Friday. And the source who told me, an old friend who was my maidservant at Woodstock and was visiting an elderly aunt in Wales and who came to visit me, told me that it was known throughout the court."

"Known? What is known?" demanded Eleanor.

Rosamund just looked at the Queen, and remained silent. She could barely bring herself to utter the words.

Suddenly the reality dawned on Eleanor. Her eyes

widened and her mouth set in a grimace.

"She is with child. Alys? She carries my husband's child. She is pregnant. Yes?"

Rosamund nodded.

Trying to restrain herself and not to show her growing fury, Eleanor decided to minimise the event until she could vent her fury when Rosamund left.

"What of it. Henry has many bastards. Some with whores, some with ladies of the court. Some he knows nothing about. He is a rampant lion, and a man such as him must be able to spill his seed into any convenient receptacle. And when he's had enough of little Alys, he will send her away, and probably give their babe to some woodsman or villager or townsman and woman to bring up as their own, accompanied by a purse of gold," she said, waving her hand dismissively.

But Rosamund remained stubbornly silent. And a reality, an unthinkable reality, began to dawn on Queen Eleanor. She blanched white, and hissed, "He is acknowledging the child as his son? That's why you're here. To beg for understanding, so that I don't blame Princess Alys."

Rosamund silently nodded.

"You're begging for my acceptance of my husband's

pregnant mistress? Yes? Which is why you're here. Tell me I'm wrong, you stupid girl. The King of England is acknowledging his child, born out of wedlock, and you expect me ... Queen Eleanor ... to forgive this affront to my standing? To my dignity? Tell me that isn't why you've journeyed here."

Rosamund said, "Highness, Princess Alys was like a daughter to me. I know in my heart that she couldn't, wouldn't, have willingly gone into King Henry's bed, had she not been forced and coerced, and had he not turned her young and innocent mind. You have, still, great influence in the Court. If you turn against Alys, she will become an object of hatred and life will be hideous, which is so wrong when blame cannot attach to a young and innocent girl. I beg of you ..."

"Get out!" Eleanor screamed. "Leave this castle, Rosamund, and never return. Go to your Nunnery and pray to God, if He'll listen. But leave me now. For if you don't, then I swear before the Almighty that your death will be hastened by many months. Now leave my presence. You are dismissed."

After she'd left, Eleanor sat trying to control her fury, and pondering the reality of the situation. Why was she so upset? Yes, Henry was having yet another baby, but that was nothing new. So why was she so annoyed and wounded? Because since her sons, young Henry, Richard and Geoffrey had risen against old Henry and been defeated, and since she'd been imprisoned two years ago, she had always been terrified that the King would disinherit her older sons and give the kingdom to John. She knew that nature ordained that she must love her youngest son, John, yet he was such a disappointment, and no matter how old Henry tried to show his fondness of the lad, he knew that of all their children, John was the one with whom he held no true love.

Yet by the rights of Kingly succession, the throne would have to be passed down to one of her sons ... unless ... even the thought made her break into a cold sweat, despite the roaring fire. Which was also the reason that her gorge had risen high enough to choke her.

She looked around at her luxurious prison, in which she was free to wander and walk the grounds, even go out for a hunt surrounded by Henry's guards.

Yet despite her freedom, she was a prisoner just as surely as she was locked in an airless dungeon with stinking shit leaking through the floor and rats running over her body to gnaw at her while she sleep. All of that she could have accepted, but not her powerlessness in this prison. And for the first time in her life, she was utterly incapable of influencing the rights of her sons over the rights of this new offspring ... assuming that the babe was a boy.

Part the SIXTH

In which the Princess Alys gives birth to a son, William, and King Henry II makes diverse promises, but is confounded by the schemes of his wife, Queen Eleanor.

———

Orford Castle Suffolk, East Anglia eight months later, May 1176

From the very beginning of her lying-in, things became starkly and totally different from the normal passage of her life up until the time of her pregnancy. She had suffered the earlier months of her pregnancy with a modicum of sickness and lethargy, but viewed it as little more than a summer cold. She was consoled and encouraged by the ever-generous and ever-present Isaac the Jew, who had now become her mentor, counsellor, and father-figure.

He trespassed on ground over which others in the

White Tower would never dare to trespass, such as how to negotiate with the King when she both wanted and needed things for her immediate and future comfort; how to tell the King, gently and with love in her heart, that she now needed rest rather than the intense and active love-making sessions they had enjoyed so much; how to select a new mistress who wouldn't present a threat to her once she entered a state of confinement; and even how to ignore the whispered barbs of the court about her being nothing more than a treasurer-seeker, a whore and a usurper.

He spent much of his time reassuring a child he viewed as he would view his granddaughter, that it was just naked jealousy which drove these vultures of the court – a term he'd picked up from the King – in their vicious and hurtful conversations, and that the substance of their hatred had nothing whatsoever to do with her. And she welcomed his daily visits, as she would welcome a visit from a grandfather, one with whom she had never been blessed.

Now huge with child, and barely able even to rise from a seat without her Ladies in Waiting assisting her, the growth of her baby had been visible to the court for months. Nobody, not Lord or Lady, had dared to comment aloud and in company of strangers, but as the young Princess's dresses had expanded in the middle ranges of her body, and the 'baby ball' became an overhanging hornets' nest above her legs, moving left and right with a life of its own, without warning, and from time to time and causing the Princess to grasp at a table or chair for stability, the whispers and corridor conversations between noble familiars, grew feverish. Whenever she walked into a room, women curtsied, men bowed, but Alys knew that when she had passed by, their faces took on grimaces and scowls of anger and hatred. For she had not only usurped Lady Rosamund, not only usurped Queen Eleanor, but this slip of a silly little French girl – princess she may be, but a nonentity in the English Court – had usurped their place in their King's mind and heart.

But remembering the advice of Rosamund to remain silent and not to inform the King, lest the families who were warned or punished for insulting her acted viciously against her, she held her counsel and merely assured the King that all was well in her life.

It was the Richard de Lucy, High Sheriff of Essex, Chief Justiciar of England, and Constable of the Tower of London who saw what was happening and decided to act. He knew Princess Alys as a charming, delightful, respectful and intelligent young woman, a favourite of his King, and bearing the Monarch's child. And having known Rosamund so well, and been told why she wouldn't tell Henry of the comments about her, Lord Richard decided to act. Rosamund had suffered greatly while he obeyed her pleas and remained silent. But this was a younger and less worldly woman, and he determined to act on her behalf.

One night, he sought private audience with the king. And man to man, ignoring that one was a supreme monarch, and he was a courtier, Lord Richard told his king of the plight which Alys was suffering. At first, Henry disbelieved it. Nobody, he said, could say such things about his beloved. Who would dare insult the King's mistress. But being Chief Justiciar, Richard was a man of impeccable honesty, and Henry was forced to listen to everything he was told.

It took Lord Richard all of his skills to quell the King's fury; it was Richard who calmed him from immediately throwing many of the court in the dungeons, and Richard who told him of the best way to deal with the situation, a manner which would be best for the Princess, and best for the Court.

Now knowing what was happening, King Henry announced the following February morning in the new year to the assembled Court, "Be it known, you Gentlemen of my court, and your Ladies, that her Royal Highness, the Princess Alys, my great and beloved friend, will leave this court, and attend her lying-in and confinement during the coming days. She will be attended by her midwives, and, also by my physician, Isaac the Jew ... and this done by my royal decree and proclamation."

At this, there was a gasp from the women who were listening. A man in the confinement room? It was unheard of. It was against God's laws and Nature itself. Yet the King of England had just announced that it would be so.

"Her Royal Highness will return to our court with our much-beloved child in the warm and peaceful months of high summer. We wish her Highness our love and God's speed for a safe and comfortable delivery. And as of this moment, My Lords and Ladies, all whispering and unseemly remarks about Princess Alys's state will cease immediately. Be aware that I know of these whispered conversations. I know who speaks them, I know who listens to them and I know who repeats them.

"So let this be my first and only warning to you noblemen and women. Instead of imprisoning and beheading the criminals and miscreants who are lying about my Princess, I will on her behalf, and at her request, utter no more than a warning. But if I am informed of any further adverse comments about my Lady from this moment onwards, then despite her speaking kindly about you and on your behalf, my sword will leave its scabbard, and God help anybody upon whom it falls. From this time forward, if any word comes to me of any unkind, unfair or undeserved remarks made by any of you about the Princess, then the utterer, and all who have listened and any who repeat them, will suffer a fate far worse than summary beheading. Because such an offence against your King deserves the cruellest of punishments. If you dare speak poison against my Lady, then you will be sent by me to the most northern regions of Scotland to spend the next many months advising on the disposition of the enemies of our nation. You will be sent without servants, without food and without money. You will fend for yourselves. Some of you may survive. But I doubt it. And so unlike beheading, which robs me of the days and weeks of joy in your suffering and robs you of the months of time you would be able to regret your folly, this punishment will last for twelve of God's months. And so, my noble men and women, may Almighty God help the miscreants who suffer this punishment, for no such help will be given by me.

"Be in no doubt about my intent. The Princess Alys is our much-beloved friend and companion, and when she is addressed, it is as though you were addressing the King! Any remarks you make about her, are remarks you would make about me. Ignore these warnings at your peril!" He sat back on his throne and was met by a wall of shock and silence.

And Alys, who was listening from an upper gallery, kept thinking of the conversation she had had all those months earlier with the Lady Rosamund, fair Rosamund, and she would have thrilled to hear those words said about herself.

After frantic preparations by horse-guards and her maidservants, a company of men rode out of the Tower of London two days later, accompanied by King Henry who rode beside his young lover. Her midwives, nurses, and Isaac the Jew had left the Castle the day before to travel by wagons to the coast of Anglia.

In the rear of the King's company, falling further and further behind, were the slow-moving wagons carrying the Princess's bed linens, her wardrobe, tapestries for the walls and window, knives, plates, carveries, dishes, and even several of the new pronged instruments which the Princess, if not the King, had become adept at using.

Normally, along with the food and drink wagons which had left the previous day, the linen and clothes and kitchen wagons would have gone ahead, but the decision to remove the Princess from the Court had been made so suddenly because of the fury of the king when he learned of the whispered remarks in corridors, that he decided to send his Lady Mistress away as swiftly as he could.

He had recently been told that similar remarks had been made behind his back against his former mistress, the Lady Rosamund Clifford, and to his horror and mounting fury, these cutting remarks had driven her to join a Nunnery and take the veil. Which was why he had agreed so readily with Lord Richard, and refused to allow Alys, younger and more innocent than Rosamund, to become prey to these scavenging vultures who made up his Court. He also decided that on his return from settling the Princess into her new confinement apartments in his newly-built Orford Castle in Anglia, that on his return, he would rid his Palace, and himself, of half the leeches and blood-suckers who contributed nothing except their desire for advancement and Royal largess, and treated their residency and attendant luxuries on his purse as their right because they were members of the Norman nobility. Their grandfathers and fathers, perhaps, had performed services to Henry's Royal forebears and they had been given precedence, but many of the peacocks who strutted his court today merely moved from their country estates to Windsor of the Tower or wherever the King resided at that time, and merely filled empty seats. They did nothing but eat and sleep, delighted in the entertainments he provided, while at the same time, made fun at his expense. Norman nobles they may well be, but soon they would be told by their Norman noble King just how wrong their assumptions had been.

But that was for his return. Right now, he had to get his love safely to her place of confinement and lying-in, ensure that the midwives and nurses and Isaac the physician would deliver his child in safety, and set a date for Alys's return to his court.

As mile after mile thundered beneath them, the Head of his Guard, Lord de Montfort, rode back, and when level with the King, asked, "Majesty, ahead by two thousand paces is a defensible hill top where I have rested my men previously. It's clear of trees, commands a high view, and is a suitable place for us to take refreshment. We'll camp there overnight, Highness, and ride on to Orford Castle on the morrow."

The king smiled. "You and your men may do that, my Lord, and you will take Her Highness with you, but I need four of your guards to accompany me a short way, about twenty miles, to the north. There I will visit my castle at Thetford, and join you the following day. I seized that castle, as well as others in the area owned by the Bigod family when they joined the insurrections against me, and punished them by destroying their seats of power. But I retained Thetford, and I wish to examine it as the summer residence for Her Highness, Princess Alys and my new child. Then she will have Woodstock and Thetford as our son's and her own castles and they will be away from the farmyard which my court is rapidly becoming."

The Lord Montfort, a large if surly man who preferred to lead an army into battle than sit and talk to courtiers in a banquet, understood immediately, asked no questions, and rode hastily forward to order four of his best soldiers to ride as a close command beside his Majesty when he left the company later in the afternoon.

The following day, without the recently departed King, when they arrived at Orford Castle, near to the town of Ipswich in the county of Suffolk. The King had decided on this castle for her confinement, because of the advice given to him by Isaac the Physician. Being close to the North Sea, the fresh air and enabling long, gentle walks while waiting for the baby to be born, would be good for her. The King had questioned the logic, telling him that the knowledge of midwives demanded that the rooms be darkened, and the pregnant Princess should do nothing but lie down and be attended by servants. The idea of walking had never been advocated by anybody who know anything about childbirth.

But Isaac had said that if he was forbidden to attend to the Princess, then this darkness and lethargy would be the situation his Lady would experience. Isaac told him of his lifetime of correspondence with the most brilliant doctors of the age, in cities far and wide on the continent, and the consensus of understanding of the human body informed him and his colleagues that such ways as the midwives practised were, indeed, harmful to the babe, and he was certain that it had led to many unnecessary deaths of both mother and child.

Isaac disagreed with the midwives, and said so firmly, as though he was teaching one of his students. He explained to the King that before castles, before knights on horseback, before the Greeks and the Romans, before the growing influence of the Mohammedans, in the days of the Jewish Bible, women had worked in the fields up to the time of delivery, given birth and then returned to their labours in less than a week. It was fresh air and easy work, not dark smoke-filled rooms and lying for week upon week on a bed, which was the best medicine. He likened the situation to a kiln. Could a beautiful pottery vase or cup be produced from a cold kiln? Surely, when a kiln was hot and fiery, it produced the most durable and beautiful pots. As it was with the human body. Give it exercise, give it good nourishment, let it be normal, and it would produce a beautiful healthy child; but let it fall into lassitude, starve it of good air and God's sunshine, and the body would sink to a low ebb, and may produce a sub-standard child.

Eventually the King had agreed, with the warning that unless the birth of his son was without risk and harm to the babe and the mother, he would be well rewarded, and his methods would become the official practise of the Court of England. But if God forbid any harm came to mother and child because of this practise, then the physician's head would be removed from his body and speared on a pikestaff above the portcullis of the Tower. Alys knew nothing of these conversations, and expected her lying-in to be as it had been explained when Isaac thought he would be excluded from the birth.

Though she was looking forward to Isaac the Jew being in attendance, and greeting her when her party arrived, as she saw it on the horizon, she looked at the Castle Orford and her heart dropped. It was little more than a tall central construction, surrounded by other towers at its edges, standing high on a hill, dominating the landscape. Unlike Windsor, Woodstock, and especially her delightful Everswell, its dominance of the country surrounding it was forbidding. Yet for the next few months, it would be where she, and soon her young son or daughter, would grow and thrive. And as they neared, to her immense delight, Isaac the Jew stood in the gateway, waving at her like an excited grandfather being greeted by his favourite granddaughter.

What both shocked and amazed the Princess for the entire time that she was in confinement, were the arguments which Isaac the Jew had with his midwives. The only thing which stopped her screaming at them to be silent in her presence, was that they were arguing vehemently and passionately about what was the best way to treat her. She knew that they all had her best interests at heart, and felt comforted, even when they were vehement in their arguments, and she thought that blood would flow at any moment.

Isaac ordered that the tapestries which they'd hung over all of the windows had to be removed. The midwives had adamantly refused, citing that the babe should feel that the entire bed chamber was an extension of the mother's womb. Isaac quoted the Old Testament of the Jews, and cited the Book of Psalms, *"You, Lord, keep my lamp burning; my God turns my darkness into light."*

"God!!!!" he shouted. "Not darkened windows. It's light which is needed so that when the babe emerges from her Highness's body, it will be welcomed into the light of the Lord and will immediately be surrounded by the luminous beauty of the world."

"Nonsense, Master," shouted back Old Judith, the most experienced of the midwives. "Babes grow in the darkness of the womb, and when they emerge, they have to be born into the dark so that they're not shocked by the brightness, and suffer a seizure. Only gently, slowly, must the babe be introduced into the glare of the day. And you talk about the luminous beauty of the world? Where is that I ask? In the shit which runs in the street? In the orphans who wonder where their next meal will come from? In the young soldiers who die on the battlefields in distant lands, yet who just want to be home with their loved ones living a peaceful life? Where is this luminous beauty of which you speak?" she demanded. When she finished speaking, the other older women nodded their heads and interjected with supportive comments.

But Isaac wasn't finished. "I am an old Jew. I have spent my life studying two things ... the Old Testament, what we call the Tenach, which is our law, the wisdom of the prophets and commentaries, and second only to this, there is my beloved art of healing through medicine. Yet that is not all of my reading, and because Christ was born a Jew, I have also studied His life in your New Testament. Even your own Apostle in this book of yours, Saint John, said, *"God is light; in him there is no darkness at all. If we claim to have fellowship with him and yet walk in the darkness, we lie and do not live out the truth."* Your Saint John, woman. Not my Saint John. He said that we should live our lives in truth, in God's light. And that includes the most innocent and guiltless of all, our babies.

"Babes should leave the darkness and safety of their mother's body when God Almighty breathes His soul into the little person, and open their hearts and mind to the eternal beauty of this world. And they do this through their eyes. Even though their eyes can barely see and comprehend the majesty of this earth, their noses, hearts and senses can experience the perfume of the fields, the scents of the flowers, the buzzing of the bees. So much beauty. You talk about soldiers dying. Yes, that is terrible, but it isn't what God ... or your Jesus ... decrees. It is what men do. Men who pervert the word of God, men who create armies and wars which make orphans and when they have raped and killed, they burn crops which leads to starvation. But who starves? The soldier? The Officer? The town's dead fathers and husbands and brothers? No, it's the women and children who aren't slaughtered by the army. It's those unable to defend themselves, who see their husbands', fathers' and brothers' bodies dismembered on the battlefield, who see the soldiers steal their crops and food, who rape their women and carry off their young as slaves ... it's these women and babes who are left alone with no crops to turn into bread and meal. To starve in the coming days.

"Yet a babe born into the light knows nothing of this and, please God, will know nothing for many years," he said. None, not his midwives nor Princess Alys, had ever seen him before in such a state. He was on the verge of tears, about to weep for the evils which beset his beautiful God-ordained and created world.

Unsure of what to do or say, and in frustration at his refusal to follow the old ways, Old Judith looked at Princess Alys, laying there, ripe with baby, and said, "Highness. It's your decision. Do you follow Master Isaac's decision and risk the health and welfare of your babe, or our way of years without number of delivering good and healthy babes into this world?"

Alys looked at both the kindly and experienced eyes of Old Judith, and then at the grandfatherly smile of Master Isaac. She thought for a moment. Unused to being judge of such decisions, she knew her next few words could be averse to one or the other. "Mistress Judith, I have listened to both of your arguments. I have great sympathy with both. But Master Isaac has treated me, comforted and advised me for many months and my trust and faith in him must prevail. Remove the tapestry from the windows, wrap me in furs against the cold, and ensure that this room is full of light so that, as the Master says, my babe will be born into the light of the Almighty and he, or she, can feel the blessings of the sun on their tender skin. There! That is my decision."

And it was done.

Despite days of sitting in the cold winter air, walking gently and with support along clifftops overlooking the grey northern sea, nothing ... nothing which Isaac said could diminish her pain. Not his reassurance, nor the demands of her King and lover who commanded that his mistress' pains had to be diminished immediately, not the crucifixes and prayer scrolls placed on her belly by the midwives ... nothing was so great that it could ameliorate the pain she experienced when her baby William was struggling to quit her body. The midwives were standing between her legs as she lay on her couch, legs spread as wide as she could, waiting to ease the babe out of her body the moment the head presented itself. They were concerned that her opening was still narrow, and wondered whether it may lead to either her death, or the crushing of her babe to save her life.

But when they whispered their concerns to Isaac the Physician, he came and looked at the opening, and merely nodded, and said, "Let Nature take its course. God knows precisely what He's doing. When God and the babe decide to pay us a visit, the little one will emerge ..." Then he looked into Alys's eyes, and mopped her brow ... "and you will open your arms to a new life."

And as if the baby heard the ministering of the physician, Old Judith suddenly said, "She's just widened. Just now, as you spoke, Master. I can see the babe's crown. It'll be here soon."

Isaac smiled, and continued to wipe Alys's brow. "See. The Lord is with us, in this room, He heard what we said, and now He is delivering our baby's crown. That means, dearest Highness, that your baby is trying to leave your body and become a child of this Kingdom."

"Is it a boy? Tell me that it's a boy," Alys gasped, trying to shut the pain out of her mind. But try as she might, a sudden spasm shot through her groin, causing her to scream loudly in a sudden paroxysm of agony.

From a distant anteroom, they heard King Henry scream out, "Relieve her pain immediately, or I'll relieve you all of your heads. This is your King who is demanding this of you. Do it now, or I shall break into the birthing room and execute you all."

The physician and midwives simply ignored the king, for they knew from experience that within a matter of half of an hour, less if God was with them, the pains would cease; in a day they'd be forgotten; and during the merriment of Christmastime, the misery and pain she was experiencing now would be lost when she began the enhancement in the laughter of the stories she told of the time when the Princess Alys gave birth to the King's son.

"Daub goose fat over the edges of Her Highness's

opening as well as just inside Her Highness's womanly passage, where you can feel the babe's head, in order to ease the passing out of the infant," Isaac ordered.

Old Judith looked at him in surprise and disagreement, but she'd been instructed to do as she was ordered by the Princess, and so she dipped her fingers into the waiting bowl of warmed fat, and smeared it on the inner lips of the girl's opening. When her fingers eased the lips apart where the babe's head was already presented, it seemed to smooth the exit, and the head appeared to … and then actually did … ease out slightly further, as though the grease had facilitated easing its journey to freedom. When there was enough head, Old Judith wiped her greasy hands on a flannel, and then grasped the head delicately to manoeuvre to so that as it exited the body, it twisted slightly to make room for the babe's shoulders to emerge.

More screams from Princess Alys, more threats of summary execution shouted by the King, more comfort from Isaac the Jew, more doubt from the midwives, and within the space of less than a quarter of the hour, a beautiful young baby slipped out of the lady's body as easily as a newly-killed rabbit being removed from its skin, and was freely born. Isaac allowed the midwives to do their work of cutting with a specially sharpened knife and knotting the cord, tying it securely, handing the baby to Isaac, then easing out the afterbirth. He looked at the child quickly to ensure that it had its God-given number of hands, feet, fingers and toes, then took the baby over to the basin, and washed the birthing matter off its eyes, cleared his ears, his nose, his mouth, and gently washed his crown and body without saying a word.

Alys, spent and utterly without any strength, in a voice as harsh as an old woman's and almost pleading, asked, "Is it a son? Have I a son? For my king?"

He looked around, and saw that Princess Alys was lying there, desperately waiting for his word. And it was his unutterable pleasure to tell her, his own voice cracking with emotion, "Be you please to learn, my Princess, that God has graced you with a beautiful, healthy little Prince. He is perfect in every way, and now needs his mother's breast."

He carried the baby boy the few steps to the birthing bed, then placed the child in his mother's open arms. Alys tried to speak, but was so full of tears and relief, that she merely sighed. She hugged her baby to her chest, and stroked its beautiful cheeks, and shoulders and face. She drew the child close to her mouth, and kissed him with the passion of a young mother but the restraint of a terrified new parent holding for the first time, a delicate new baby's toy.

"And now, Highness, it is my duty to go and inform my King that his beloved friend has delivered him a healthy son," he said, bowing and retreating out of the room.

Before the midwives helped the baby onto Alys's breast, they teased its mouth with their finger, covered in some breast milk they'd extracted from Alys that morning. And as always happened, the baby frowned, then licked the new white liquid with its tongue, and continued licking. But soon the licks gave way to the babe's lips pursing, seeking more and the place from where the food had come. He began to whimper again, which caused the midwives to smile.

They did this so that the baby knew and was familiar with the taste of its mother's milk and could begin immediately sucking when placed on her breast. They knew, from experience, the trauma and guilt a mother would experience if a babe rejected the teat. Also, their actions had made the babe cry, which was good for his breathing. He would cease crying the moment he was placed on the mother's breast. So they led him to her, ensured that his mouth was secured on her nipple, tickled his foot to make him react and begin the suckling motions, and saw with pleasure that the little boy knew precisely what it do.

Now that he was suckling properly, they covered him with warm blankets, and were then free to clear up the birthing room in preparation for the immediate arrival of the King. But the arrival of his voice happened at that moment from a distant room, when they all looked up in amusement as they heard Henry's stentorian voice scream out, "WHAT! A Boy. A SON! I have a son with the woman I love! I've given the world a son. Praise be to God in the highest. A boy. Out of my way. I'm going to see my good and loyal son!"

The Oxford Parliament (known as the Mongrel Parliament) May 1177

The greatest lords of England had gathered to hear the King's proclamation, to be present as their Majesty informed them of the future of their realm, to know who would be their new king, and how their fortunes may or may not be affected by old King Henry's demise. Although he had been made co-Monarch years ago, young Henry was regarded with little or no respect as their noble's overload, as all power had been retained in the old lion's paws. They paid him lip-service, called him 'majesty' and bowed when they were in his presence, but smirked behind his back; and if he ever gave an order to be obeyed, they would immediately question it with the old King.

Because old Henry, still robust, still hale, still a fearsome ruler of men and lands, still the greatest commander of forces in all Christendom, was their true and anointed king, whatever sophistry and device the young pretender had used to elevate half of his arse onto the throne. Yet despite all of his strength and prowess, old Henry was showing the signs of his mortality. Grey haired, now stooped, slower in body if not mind, his voice harsher than it had been even two years earlier, he had personally welcomed all of the Barons and Earls, Lords and Knights to his Great Council in the town of Oxford, a festival of discussion and instruction which he called his Parliament that evening. He'd chosen Oxford as it was a scholastic town full of reverend teachers and priests, far from any other large town or city, far from the estates of most of his Councillors, yet close enough to London so that the King didn't have to travel too far.

His Lady, the Princess Alys hadn't attended the evening banquet to welcome the Lords, as she was in attendance of the king's one year old son, still being wet-nursed, but happily laughing now and playing with both mother and father. He already had many words and was teetering around on his chubby little legs.

In truth, much as King Henry enjoyed the company of his Lords and Esquires, he was no longer the king of old, a man who would drink and carouse around a roaring fire of elm or beechwood until the early hours of the morning, then sleep until sunrise, storm out of bed screaming instructions to his sluggish servants who'd quickly dress and feed him prior to his morning's hunt. But these days, both because age was catching up with him, and because he so loved the company of his mistress Alys and the hilarious antics of his little son William, he preferred to retire immediately after the banquet, return to his privy chambers and spend the night in the gentle loving amiable company of his *de facto* wife and son. Yet in truth, though his well-begotten son, he was more William's grandsire than father.

Yet on this night, after the Oxford Parliament banquet to welcome the company of Councillors, the King returned to his chambers, leaving his Lords to carouse and enjoy their festivities. As he entered the bed chamber, he saw the young and beauteous Alys, hugging the recently fed

William, kissing their little son, throwing him up in the air to the squeals and delights of the innocent child, and utterly oblivious to the custom of almost every other noble lady with a little babe. Others did their best to ignore their children, and not allow them to interfere with the commerce of their lives as noble women; that had been the case to his certain knowledge with the women he'd known best in his own life, his mother Matilda, and his wife Eleanor, who were barely known to their children until they had become young adults and capable of ruling a company of soldiers.

Alys, on the other hand, was unafraid of being seen as a devoted mother; she cared not a whit for what people said of her. She loved their William with a strength and intensity which was a God-given delight. Just as she loved her *de facto* husband King Henry of England and Aquitaine.

Even the Lords and Ladies of his court, even his sons young Henry, Richard, Geoffrey and John grudgingly acknowledged that she was no strumpet trying to pave a wealthy road ahead for herself. The love, care and devotion which Alys showed to Henry was beyond anything which any of Eleanor's children had ever experienced, and when they looked at the transparent devotion she showed when in Henry's company and when mother and father were playing with their new child, it was evident that this was a match of love. They looked carefully for signs of falsity, for hidden grimaces, for gossip between her and her maidservants; but there was none. Either she was performing a role to a level they had never previously experienced, or she was genuinely, deeply, passionately in love with old Henry. And if that was the case, it was a love beyond lust, beyond desire, beyond the satisfaction of a carnal need; it was a deep and passionate love, one of which none of the sons had any experience.

Their father and mother had described the love and devotion which old Henry had shown to Eleanor in the early years of their marriage, while they were creating the next generation of rulers in their sons and daughters; but never of the way in which they had described their passion for each other, had they touched on aspects of tenderness, devotion, playfulness, happiness. Never had old Henry nor Eleanor described their love for each other in terms which their sons had understood as anything more than unbridled lust, desire and fulfilment.

Yet what had resulted from old Henry's devotion to his wife Eleanor and their brood? What had come of the lust and passion, the fire and the fury of those first days of their marriage, when he was nineteen, and she was a matron of thirty years? Eleanor was now imprisoned, held firmly in her castle and its grounds by silken threads and doubtless plotting her next uprising. And her sons, other than weak and pathetic John, had rebelled against their father and been forced to prostrate themselves to beg for forgiveness; it had been grudgingly given, but the seeds of another uprising and rebellion were growing by the day; his beloved mistress Rosamund had died in agony, dressed in the veil of a nun, yet as far from God as any woman in history; and now of all of the people who had lived with old Henry in his life, the one who remained standing, the one who had somehow raced to supremacy in front of the pack, was the one least worthy, and least expected. Princess Alys! Now the mother of the king's latest bastard, now the woman warming his bed ... and now the mistress who was dominating his mind and thoughts.

But for this Council meeting in Oxford, this Parliament of Lords and other nobles, most of his sons were absent ... by his command. Only John of Eleanor's sons, was present, and his presence wouldn't be acknowledged until the following morning, when old King Henry would make his great announcement.

He stood for long moments at the entry to the bed

chamber, hidden by the doorway from Alys and young William. Only the departing wetnurse saw him as she was leaving. She started to curtsey, but he silently motioned her not to do anything but leave, as he wanted to observe his mistress and their son playing innocently together. It was as though their closeness was generating waves of love and warmth which enveloped the entire room. And as an observer, he took great delight in just standing there, after the noise and laughter of the banqueting hall, and listening to the soft, loving and motherly sounds which were so strange to his ears.

He made no sound, yet Alys suddenly grasped William tightly as she turned and looked towards the doorway.

"Henry? Majesty? Are you there?" she asked softly. "Love? Husband? Come to your William. He wants to bid you goodnight."

Henry beamed a smile and entered the room. "I took great pleasure in just observing you. You didn't know, but the sight of you playing with our son warms my old heart. Dear God, Alys, but I love you and our little boy."

He walked over, took a goblet of wine from the table, and sat beside her. Knowing him as well as she did, Aly realised immediately that there was a weighty issue playing on his mind.

"You're troubled, my Liege?" she said.

"No. Nothing. A trifle."

"Henry? Tell me and I'll ease your burden," she said softly, handing their son over to him. William sat on his knee and beamed a smile when he reached up and tried to touch Henry's white beard. Then the child's hands stretched further to touch his nose. Henry immediately opened his mouth and pretended to swallow the little boy's hand, which caused the babe to howl in laughter.

Alys reached across, and stroked Henry's leg. "What troubles you, Henry?"

He breathed deeply. It was a conversation that he knew he had to have with her. It related to her security after his death, and most especially to the safety of their son. But William wasn't his only son, and the laws of primogenitor were sacrosanct. God's Laws. The Laws of Nature.

"Tomorrow, dearest Alys, I will be announcing decisions concerning the disposition of my realms here in England, in Ireland, and in Aquitaine. I will announce them to the Lords and Nobles of my Council. From that moment onwards, it will be the law of the land, irrefutable, irredeemable." And then he sighed deeply and seemed to retract into his own body.

"Good!" she said. "These things have to be discussed and decided. We are all mortal. All of us will die. The question is what we will leave for those whom we have brought into this world. So how does this affect your son William?"

"I have many sons, Alys. William, though my much beloved child, with a woman I view as my wife in all but name, is still a bastard, and as such, though he will be cared for all his life as the son of a King, he cannot, will not, be a part of my inheritance. You must have realised that this would be the case. I have many bastard children, and all are cared for by Ladies of my court or widows or spinsters on my estate ... even by members of my staff. I give purses of gold each year to ensure their good upbringing. But the one thing I can never do is to acknowledge them. The only sons I can acknowledge are my sons by Queen Eleanor, Henry, Richard, Geoffrey and John. Henry is my co-regent, although this bastard son, as with the others, rose against me, and is still doing penance. Richard and Geoffrey similarly rose against me, but despite their treason, despite the enmity they feel towards me, thanks to my Queen Eleanor, I have to name my sons as dukes of my provinces. Only John stood by me, young and unkingly as he is and, God help us, ever will be. Yet he is known far and wide as *Johan sans Terre* – John Lackland. There has been no territory, until now, that I could will and bequest to him as his inheritance. Yet that is no longer the case.

"My purpose for calling this parliament of my nobles, is to inform them of my decision that I will be making Prince John into the King of Ireland, which I am entitled to do because of a Bull called Laudabiliter, issued over twenty years ago by the English Pope Adrian. In that Bull, the Pope grants me the right to invade and govern Ireland. Which I have done, and now part of that festering bogland is mine, and soon the entire island will be English. And John will be its first king. Then my sons, those of my sons by Queen Eleanor, will have their lands, and I will die knowing that my *imperium* is secure for generations of Plantagenet kings to come."

Alys sat quietly for some moments, absorbing what the king had just said. She already knew what was going to happen. She had predicted it the month of William's birth and had formulated a plan which she would soon have to discuss with Henry. She had bided her time, initially because she wanted to make Henry fell in love with her, which he had done; yet remarkably, despite the difference in their ages, she too had fallen in love with the old King. It came as a surprise one night, when he was off at war, leading an Army somewhere. But she realised that while she was sewing a part of a small tapestry, she was actually thinking about him; in part as her father, her protector, yet also as her lover, the man who had taken her innocence, and not squandered it. Who had shown her kindness, love, tenderness; who had listened to her while she spoke, sought her counsel on matters concerning the household; the man who sought her out to go hunting with him, and who seemed to absorb her youth and adventure and spirit when his own were flagging and low.

Yet despite this, despite knowing that she would soon have to talk about the safety of herself and her son when he passed heavenly, when the words came from his mouth, it was still a shock to hear how she and her son, beloved with all his heart, were soon to be abandoned by the King.

For the better part of a year, a year of growing happiness and love, a year of devotion to her son and her lover, Alys hadn't closed her eyes to his age, his death, and the condition she would find herself in when it happened.

How safe would her son William be from the naked hatred of Richard and Geoffrey, let alone young Henry? How secure would she be? Would she suddenly find herself turned out of the Palace the moment Henry was dead? Would Queen Eleanor, festering and fuming in her prison, come roaring back to life, fired with the intensity of an avenging angel, an Old Testament prophetess come to judge those who had abused her, wildly swinging a battle-ax cutting a swathe through all those who had sided with old Henry against her? Would Richard wreak his ultimate revenge, do as he'd tried to do in Aquitaine, and plunge a sword into her breast? How could, how would she protect her son William if she was dead?

For all his hatred of his and Eleanor's sons, old Henry was more determined to secure his legacy as a great King of England and Aquitaine than he was to ensure the safety of Alys and her son. And now the moment of her truth had arrived. He was about to abandon her and his son to the fortunes of the most turbulent family in the entire history of humanity. And that was one thing which Princess Alys, daughter of the King of France, *de facto* wife of the King of England, mother of a future king, was determined would never ever happen. The only person who could ensure her future was herself, and now was the time to put her ideas into practice.

Unlike when he'd been drinking all night, and he came to her in a state of exhaustion and inebriation, tonight he had drunk mildly, and was delighting in the antics of his son William.

So now was, perhaps, the time to begin the discussion. Not the whole discussion, but just the beginning. For if he were to accept the idea she had formulated, then she was wise enough to know that when it eventually came to him, probably when he woke with the idea in his mind, it would have to have been his idea ... not hers. For then he would ensure its success, then it would be beyond criticism of his courtiers, and the only battles he would have to fight were with his sons, and, of course, his Queen Eleanor.

"Majesty ... Henry ..."

He looked up from William's antics, still smiling because of the little chubby boy. "Yes, my love."

"How long do you intend to keep your Queen, Eleanor, in prison?"

"While so ever that viper has breath in her body. Or when the breath leaves my body and others are in control of her fate," he said, suddenly tickling William under his armpit and making the little boy squeal in joy.

"Sire, husband, wouldn't it be a fairer thing to do to allow her freedom? At her age? How much longer can she continue to enjoy her life? Let her be free these last remaining years."

Henry looked at her in amazement. "Let her free? Would you let a nest of hornets free in a banqueting room? Would you let a bear walk free throughout the castle, killing and maiming every person in sight? Are you mad? Allow Eleanor her freedom? Dearest, the moment that embittered old woman, that feisty nag, that miserable sagweed in silks is released, she will breathe in the air of vengeance and raise an army from the Holy Roman Emperor, the King of France, the King of Spain and God only knows where else, and I will be attacked on every border in my realm. To free her would be the greatest disaster of my reign."

"Not if you annulled your marriage before she was released and sent her back to Paris, Majesty. She would have no claim on you, your lands, and as you are crowned monarch of Aquitaine it need not be returned to her. Let the King of France negotiate that. As to the grounds for the annulment, they could be that she used force or fear to obtain your consent to her marriage. She was fleeing your brother Geoffrey, and she forced you to marry her to save her. I believe that his Holiness, Pope Alexander, would annul the marriage on those grounds, as you were coerced into marriage by the fear she instilled in you to save and protect her."

Then cleverly, Alys looked away from Henry, reached over and tickled her William, as though the scheme she'd just told the King was a mere after-thought.

But Henry sat quietly, staring into the distance. "But if the Pope, not that I think he would …"

"He would if you doubled the Annates payable to Rome for this year … and next …"

" … if he would, surely that annulment has the effect of our never having been married," he said softly. "And then all of our children together would be bastards …"

She fought back a smile, and said softly, "Like William…

Even his closest nobles, those who had been his friends and hunting partners for all of his life, couldn't understand why His Majesty showed such little pleasure in announcing the grant of an overlordship of Ireland to his youngest son, John. Though the lad was only ten years old, it was necessary for him to be granted a title which eventually would become a Kingship, albeit under the suzerainty of his brother, young King Henry.

Yet when the nobility of England was assembled

in the great hall to hear the King's Oxford Parliament announcement, and despite the cheers and huzzahs from the assembly, despite the look of unutterable joy and bursting pride in Prince John's young face … despite all of that, there was a look of detachment in old King Henry's eyes. Most failed to notice it, when he stood, picked up the kneeling boy after he'd kissed the King's ring finger, hugged him, and raised his fist into the air.

The young Prince and future king of Ireland beamed, Old Henry beamed … yet those who knew Henry best saw that the only thing on his face which carried no joy, were his eyes. And they found it strange. For of all his rebellious treasonous malicious querulous sons, only John had stayed loyal to his father; despite his youth and unkingly manner, only John was deserving of elevation into the ranks of real monarchy. Only John.

Yet there was no pride in old Henry's eyes. No feelings of warmth and relief that at last, part of his bequests, part of his inheritance, was settled.

He still had to deal with the precipitate demands of young Henry, of the still unmarried Richard and Geoffrey, and especially of the venomous fangs of Queen Eleanor. But these were matters which the old king would put to rest in the coming months. For the moment, his most pressing matter, *Johan sans Terre,* had been laid to rest. John Lackland no more. Now the old king could look towards the disposition of the rest of his territories.

Yet! Yet those closest to the old king knew that there was a look of deep and unrequited thought in his eyes; the look of a man who had just seen a road which divided into two paths, and he was uncertain as to which one led to a bottomless bog, and which to the city of Jerusalem on a hill. When the company of nobles had dispersed and sought out food and drink in the nearby banqueting hall, one of old Henry's closest friends, Baron Turstin FitzRolf, went and secured two goblets of Rennish wine, and carried them into the Parliament Room. He gave one to Henry, who took it gratefully, and then quaffed the entire goblet without a breath.

"Another, Sire?" asked Turstin.

He put the goblet down on the table, wiped his mouth and shook his head. "It quenched my thirst. I thank you, Sir Baron."

"Sire, we've known each other, boy and man, much of our lives. My grandsires and yours took this country from the Saxons. There's little you don't know about me, and with great and abiding humility, Sire, there's little I don't know about you. So as is my habit of a lifetime, and God spare me if I offend you, I have to say that the bequest of a kingship of Ireland to the young Prince John, seemed to please all but you. If there's a question which needs to be raised, but in complete privacy, my ear is yours and my wisdom is at your disposal."

Henry smiled, and thanked his friend. "But unless your name has recently changed from Turstin to Solomon, then not even you and your wisdom can assist me in my thoughts."

"My old wet nurse, who died many years hence, told me that if you share a trouble with a friend, even if there is no solution, then the misery of that trouble is halved. Would talking the trouble through assist you in finding a solution?" he asked, as gently and unobtrusively as he could.

Henry thought for a long moment, and said, "Do you return to your estates today? Or could you return in the morrow? For if you have time, come and dine with me and my mistress Princess Alys tonight. In our privy dining chamber. I will share our problem, and seek your counsel. But I swear to you, old friend, that if one word finds its way beyond our chamber, it will be the last word you ever speak. Our friendship might have lasted a lifetime, but you will find that the King's business is fatal if the words come from the wrong mouth."

Knowing the risks to his life and liberty, Baron Turstin FitzRolf approached the King's privy chambers later that evening. The sun had been set for several hours, yet the blaze of torches along the corridors and the sentries posted at strategic places enabled him to find his way easily. But though he and old Henry had spent much of their lives chasing whores around towns and villages in England and France, even though they'd shared many different women, even though they'd woken up from drunken revelries late in the morning, Turstin felt a sense of dread as he stood before the King's guards in front of the privy chamber. The Captain, who knew the Baron as well as he knew his own brother, nodded in deference, turned and knocked on the door. With every bang, Baron Turstin's heart beat louder. Today could spell his end if he gave advice which offended the king's ear; or it could spell the confiscation of his lands and banishment for his entire family. Old Henry was in a mood where anything, and everything, untoward, could happen.

The captain pushed open the door; Turstin entered the well-lit chamber, and was suddenly alone with the old King, his young and beautiful mistress, and their giggling little boy William. It was a shock. The only times he had viewed old Henry with any members of his family, had been just before, during or in the aftermath of a vicious quarrel. Voices were always raised, words shouted, sarcastic remarks hissed under breath, faces wizened in scowls of hatred.

Yet as he stood at the entry to the King's privy chambers, Turstin witnessed a scene of family bliss, a tapestry of eternal happiness; the old King was lying on the floor with his one year old babe straddling his stomach, being bounced in the air, giggling and laughing in the utter innocence of a child. His beautiful young mistress, lean and svelte, womanly yet innocuous lay beside them as would any wife or mother, holding the little lad's hand to steady him so that he didn't fall off his father's stomach, whispering soft and loving words to them both.

Old Henry noticed Turstin's entry and waved to him. "Ah, dear old friend. Though you've met them many times, may I introduce the most wonderful and loving woman and babe ever given to this world by Almighty God. This, my Lord Baron, is true happiness. This is what fatherhood should be for all my subjects."

Before he could say a word in response, the Princess Alys said, "And this is what motherhood and childhood should be in the very best of families. A loving and devoted father who nurtures and plays with his baby, a mother who is there to comfort and cherish her child...a family who values the God-given joys of this life from which Noah and his family saved us all after the Flood."

"Indeed, Majesties," said Turstin. "And you do make a truly inspiring and devoted family."

Handing his son over to Alys, Henry roused himself from the floor, stood, and said, "Come, let's eat. I'm starving. The afternoon's hunt provided us with game bird."

They all gathered around the table, beside which on the buffet, platters of food and jugs of wine had been places. Collecting trenchers, the two men filled their plates with meat and leaves, while Alys kissed her baby, gave him to Henry to kiss goodnight, and then handed little William to one of her maids to take to his cradle.

They sat around the table, and the old King said to Alys, "Madam, I informed you that Baron Turstin, one of my oldest and most trusted friends, would join us tonight. But I didn't tell you why. During the Investiture of my son John this morning as Overlord of Ireland, the Baron noticed that my heart, truly, wasn't present at the ceremony. Only he, I suspect, noticed, for all my nobles and councilmen were pleased that *Johan sans Terre* now has both land and an inheritance. Yet Turstin saw in my eyes that not all was at ease in my mind, and has come, as my oldest and best friend, to ease my conscience.

"For this reason, Madam, I have decided to tell him those matters which have been troubling me, and to see if we two ... we three ... can reach a solution to a problem which I perceive as insoluble," the King said. Then he turned to his servants, and ordered more wine to be poured.

Alys already knew of the purpose of Turstin's visit. Of all Henry's old friends, he was the only one who accorded her respect, not just because she was the king's mistress and mother of his latest child, but because he seemed to have genuine affection for her, and had often sought her out for nothing more than a friendly talk.

"The question is," said the King, "where to begin ..."

"Perhaps, Sire, you could begin with your Queen, Eleanor, and your sons who to this day remain in a state of fury and agitation about their inheritance. For without knowing the true reason for your seeking my counsel, I make the assumption that this morning's investiture has opened the gates to the situation with your other sons," he said. Knowing that he was treading on very thin ice, he held his breath, waiting for the king's response.

But the old man nodded. "It occurred to me, and this is why these matters will stay at this table ..." Suddenly Henry realised that there were servants in the periphery of the room, and peremptorily ordered them all to leave, " ... that there is one solution. The only solution. It came to me one night, yet the consequences are too dangerous to contemplate ..."

"An annulment from the Queen?" asked Baron Turstin quietly.

Shocked, both old Henry and Alys looked at the Baron, as though he'd just uttered the forbidden name of God.

"How ... but ..." stuttered Alys.

Baron Turstin smiled. "Majesties, do you think that we counsellors, your friends, just come here to shout huzzah and eat and drink and carouse? We spend our time debating the issues which afflict this court and others, and how best to advise our King to his great advantage on his great matters. Marriages might be made in Heaven, Sire, but contracts are made between men, and in the right circumstances, can be fractured.

"You married Queen Eleanor many years ago and have produced a stable of fine young men and women. But some of the men, your sons, have turned against you, jealous, anxious for advancement, wanting power before their time. And all of this instigated by her Royal Highness, the Queen of these lands.

"By God's laws and the laws of Nature, by primogenitor and the inheritance of kings, the throne on your passing should go to your eldest still living child. Young King Henry. Baronetcies and Dukedoms may be assigned under him by you, but on your death, young Henry, as King, may dispose of them as he sees fit.

"But therein lies a problem for yourself, your mistress Alys and your son William. For the moment you die, and young Henry becomes king, what of Eleanor? Now safe, she won't remain a prisoner for more than the blink of an eye when you are constricted to the confines of a grave. And God help the Lady Alys ... and more especially, God help the bastard Prince William."

Alys was still too stunned to speak, but Henry seemed to listen to every word, and responded immediately. "Yes, yes, that's the problem. But I've called you here for the solution. As I said this morning, my Lord Baron, I will officially dub you Solomon if you can solve this issue."

"Solutions are easy, Majesty. But the consequences of those solutions will become very hard to live with. The best and only solution is to petition Pope Alexander III to annul the marriage. Grounds can easily be found," said Turstin.

"I've thought about that, and it seems a good idea," said Henry. "It seems the only way. Then I can send old Eleanor off to Paris or even Aquitaine. I would lose a province if it meant peace for my realm. And that old nag would be satisfied with Aquitaine if she had her freedom."

"But there is still the problem of your sons, my King," said Turstin. "Henry needs and seeks power. The title you've given him of young King won't satisfy him if his noblemen and women bow and nod and smile when he gives an order, yet when his back is turned, seek you out for your approval. And Richard is like a castle door banging in a gale. He wants to rule a land and its peoples in order to feel the power of leadership. He wants to exercise the ultimate supremacy of life and death over all the subjects in his domain. But how safe are chickens from a fox? And after his highness Richard, we come to Geoffrey. Like a coiled snake waiting for his chance to strike, he lies there viewing the land and those who walk it, seeking advantage, opportunity, and waiting to strike and sink his fangs into any over whom he will gain advantage. He is quiet but all the more menacing.

"As to which is the most dangerous of your sons,

my Liege, I would have to say each and every one, save your best and most beloved, Prince John, is a direct and immediate threat to my Lady Alys and your son William."

Irritably, old Henry said, "Yes! All this I know. I have grown and nurtured this snake pit all their festering lives. All this I know, Sir Baron, but what is my solution? What to do?"

"Annulment of your marriage to Queen Eleanor is your only way forward, Majesty. As though it had never happened. Cite consanguinity or threats or whatever reason you can in order to convince the Pope to accede. He'll do what he's told provided you pay handsomely. Then marriage to the woman you truly love the Princess Alys who, because of the vacancy, will become queen of England. Disinheritance of all your and Eleanor's children. Even John, for whom you can make subsequent arrangements. Then young Henry, Richard and Geoffrey will lose their rights to titles. Only John may be saved, for he can be adopted as Queen Alys's right and lawful son. During William's minority, there will be a regency under Queen Alys, guided by her council of Elders to ensure the welfare of the kingdom after your death, and before the young Prince's majority and ability to rule England and Aquitaine, Ireland and, in the coming years, Scotland," said Turstin.

"Impossible!" growled Henry.

Alys merely sat back, too stunned to speak. She thought she was the only person to have conceived of this plot, yet Baron Turstin had just espoused that which had been playing around in her mind for weeks and weeks.

"Impossible!" Henry growled again. "Do you not think that these thoughts haven't been rattling around like rusted chains in my mind all these weeks? The moment I annul my wedding to Eleanor, I will be attacked by every army on God's own earth … the French, the Italians, the Prussians, the Spaniards, the Portuguese … they'll all stand on their clifftops and look over to the lunacy of England; and then they'll come seeking me out when they sniff the air and see the festering mess that my realm has become."

"Majesty," said Turstin, "that may happen. Or if you station armies on your southern shores and show your strength, they will think again and retreat, as the cowards they are. But one thing will certainly happen unless you take action. Your sons, under the tutelage of Queen Eleanor, have all revolted once, save that good lad of yours, Prince John. Your treasonous sons are now back in your fold, kneeling and grovelling. But how long can dogs be chained before they try to free themselves?

"Today they realise the gravity of their errors. But for how long will this memory last, Majesty? Richard has a fearsome temper and will rouse himself when the wind blows against him. Ambition seeps out of young Henry's skin like a festering wound. And Geoffrey sits on the sideline of any battle, and waits to see which victor he should support ... or whether he could become the ultimate victor, striding over the dead bodies.

"Word has it that that Richard and Geoffrey are already restive and eager to rise up against you again. Henry looks to the King of France for an army and support. Eleanor is said to be sending messages to the rulers of nations via her visiting priests and bishops; she is pleading for them to come to her aid, to free her so that she can join battle against you. Though you have forbidden them to see her, she is still able to speak through intermediaries to her sons Henry, Richard and Geoffrey, goading them to rise up against you once more.

"So what, Sire, do you imagine could be worse that the *status quo*? Would it be worse to remain as you are and fight another treasonous insurrection led against you by these self-same sons. Or would it be better to cut off the viper's head? Quit your marriage to Eleanor.

Disinherit those traitorous sons who would stick a sword in your gullet? Give your kingdoms over to the son who laughs and plays on your lap with all the love and innocence God had provided, and with a devoted and loving mother to guild him in the ways of Kingship? My Liege, beloved Henry, my King, I have known and adored you all my life. This is my counsel. I live and die by my advice," the Baron Turstin said, and then slumped back in his chair, as though suddenly emptied of all vigour, and remained quiet.

Henry too sat back in his chair, and picked up a slice of lamb in his fingers, which he chewed while thinking.

Alys didn't dare to interrupt him, even though the Baron's thoughts were in precise alignment with her own. It was almost as though he was reading her mind. She looked at Baron Turstin, and realised that he, too, was looking at Henry, wondering if these were to be the last moments of his life on Earth.

But Henry nodded, and said, "Like all good solutions to problems, Turstin, yours is simple and straightforward. But that doesn't make it cither easy, or right. To divorce Eleanor would be matter of difficulty and negotiation with the Pope, but I dare say it could be done. Yes, a handful of armies would seek me out to end me, but I've dealt with invading armies all my life, and even in my old age, they don't worry me. But to annul her, to say that we had never been married. To disinherit my flesh and blood …"

"Flesh and blood, Sire, which has turned against you; which tried to disinherit you; which did everything in its power to overthrow and kill you. Is that the flesh and blood to which you refer …" said the Baron.

And before he could respond, Turstin continued, "… and what if they had succeeded, my King? What if great Henry were no more, and in his place was Young King Henry, defeated in battle, untested in kingship, unproven in government? Or young King Richard, who shares only your temper, but not your skills? Or King Geoffrey, a goodly lad as friend and fellow-drinker, but as a son, and were he to be Monarch of these Isles …?

"Would the Barons and Earls, the Lords and Knights bow to these youths as they bow to you, obey these usurpers as they presently obey you, bend their knees in reverence as they walk past, as we do lovingly and willingly to you this day? Would there be harmony after your death, or will there be chaos, baron fighting baron, knight fighting knight? And what will prevent the kings of France or Spain, Portugal or Italy massing on our borders and taking advantage of the quarrels which will naturally erupt once these proud sons of yours fight each other in order to own your legacy? Nothing. England and Aquitaine will devolve into the worst chaos seen since William of Normandy sailed over the sea to conquer these lands."

Part the SEVENTH

Everswell one-week later June 1177

She had never known him to be so quiet, so thoughtful and pensive, indeed so withdrawn from his usual appetite for life. Since arriving at Woodstock after the Oxford Parliament, Henry had become a different man. Quiet, contemplative, like Atlas with the weight of the world on his shoulders. Most of his staff, caught by surprise by their sudden appearance, couldn't see the difference in the old man, but Alys could.

Certainly this was the case with her, as well as his friends, if not with others. When in his normal state, he filled the void with his presence, but today and since his dinner with the Baron, it was as though he had transmuted from warrior king to philosopher king. When they were together, Alys looked closely at him as he stared into the distance, almost as though he was thinking about another woman. He looked at her, kissed her, hugged her, but she knew that though his body was present, his mind was elsewhere. With his servants, he was quick, abusive and short-tempered, and knowing the King's moods, they kept a wary distance. With Alys, he was kindly and gentle, but she knew that a part of him was withdrawn.

It had all resulted from his dinner with the Baron Turstin FitzRolf. Now, old Henry was behaving as though a part of him was still at the dinner table, debating and discussing how to dispose of his problems. He was still the old Henry to unfamiliar observers, but to those like Alys who knew and loved him so well, it was as though the vitality had vapourised from his soul like a pool of water on a hot day.

Leaving Oxford the day following the Parliament seemed to lift his spirits somewhat, and on the journey towards London, he'd ridden ahead of his guards with Alys and talked lovingly about his joy in her as his true wife, and his son William as the light of his heart. So enamoured did he seem that when they were not five miles south of the city gates of Oxford, Henry surprised everybody by suddenly stopping his horse, ordering most of his guards to return to London, and a smaller contingent to remain with him and Alys while they turned their horses north in order to take up residency in Woodstock.

Yet for all their loving, their tenderness, his unutterable joy in little William, part of him was still at the dinner in Oxford. For the week they'd been in residence, they'd hunted, ridden, danced, been entertained by minstrels and jongleurs, as well as a troop of actors who happened to be travelling from Oxford to the North of England. Deliberately, she had refrained from mentioning the topic which was obviously pressing on his mind, but as he seemed to withdraw more and more from her she knew that she would have to broach the subject, or a curtain would be drawn over it, and then she would have no participation in his decision. And the lives of both herself and her son William depended on her ability to control his thoughts and actions.

She chose her time cautiously. They had recently returned from an afternoon hunt, and killed a magnificent deer, which his cooks would butcher and serve them that night for dinner. Returning to Everswell, Princess Alys ordered a tub to be brought into the hall, and filled with warm water. When the King had attended to business in Woodstock, he crossed the short divide over the bridge and entered Everswell. To his surprise as he entered their chambers, he saw his bath already prepared before a fire, even though it was in mid-summer.

"What's this, my love?" he asked Alys.

"Majesty, after the hunt and before dinner, I have prepared a bath for your person. It will be my honour and delight to bathe you. I have soaps from Italy and perfumes from France and tonight, we will wash away the odours of the day and you will be refreshed and ready for a night of love. I have had my maids set out your dining clothes in my bed chamber, in readiness for your Highness."

The king beamed a smile, and was about to say something, but instead merely stood there in appreciation of the delights of what had been done for him. He shook his head, as though he was seeing a wondrous flight of angels for the first time in his life.

"Madam, you are wife, mother, daughter, mistress and lover. Your kindness makes my heart burst with joy and pride."

He walked into the room, where his servants curtsied and then immediately helped him remove his chains of office and his jerkin so that he stood before the large vat of warm water in his trews and undershirt. Alys looked at him, and especially his body, now partly visible through the flimsy fabric.

She then ordered her servants to leave the room, and close the door so that they were alone. Then she undid the King's remaining clothes and when he was naked, helped him ascend the ladder so that he could climb into the large tub.

When his body was hidden, she clapped her hands, and a maidservant entered the room. Quickly she helped Princess Alys remove all of her clothes, and then assisted her to climb the ladder and enter the water barrel to stand beside her lover. The maid handed her a flannel and soaps, and for the next minutes, Alys washed those parts of the king's body which she could reach without submerging her head under water. The king, utterly thrilled by the warmth of the water, the erotic smells of the perfumed soap and the attention he was receiving from the woman he loved with all his heart, merely stood there and revelled in the attention.

Henry, who washed and bathed his entire body every two weeks, had never smelled soap of this kind before. Normally made from animal fats which stank, this soap, which Alys told him was imported by her from the Soapmaker's Guilds of Spain, was based on olive oil and

Andalusian flower perfumes, and simply delightful. And he allowed her, willingly, to attend to every part of his body, as a sculptor seeks out the true inner lines of beauty from a lump of marble.

They remained, naked and closely together in the warm water, until she felt that the king needed to sit and rest. Clapping her hands again, a male member of the King's entourage walked in, and assisted the King out of the bath. He swathed the monarch of England in a large linen towel so that the king's nakedness was covered. Then left the chamber so that one of the Princesses' ladies in waiting could enter and assist her out of the barrel. They dried before the fire, and then servants entered in order to dress both of them.

Now clean and dressed, Princess Alys looked over at the king while his servants fussed with his clothes and chains. When she'd been a little girl, he had towered above her and she'd been intimidated by his size, the strength of his voice, his gruff and aggressive manner and his seeming lack of affection. Her memory from those days of her childhood were of a man shouting all the while, of people cowering in fear should he walk into a room, and of his children huddling in corners, whispering in secret about things which seemed terrifying. There was a constant atmosphere of fear, intimidation and secretiveness within the walls of the Castles and Palaces where they lived, and it infused her sense of who she was, and where life had thrust her.

And as she absorbed the anger and mistrust, hatreds and fears of family and courtiers whenever King Henry was present, so Alys, too, had spent many days and nights hiding in fear of him. This was especially true when his voice, as so often it was, rose to a shout or when he was little more than a thunderstorm threatening the lives of those in his presence. It could be heard reverberating around the walls and corridors of the palaces, and when she heard it, she would run to her chambers.

But when she grew up, when she was already a young and marriageable woman, when she was cast out by Richard who didn't want to marry her and there seemed no place for her in life, and when Henry first noticed her in Windsor Castle as a lady and no longer a girl, she suddenly and surprisingly saw him differently, too. She remembered the very moment it happened.

It had been early in a morning, and she was preparing to go out for a ride, when she walked through the banqueting hall to quell her hunger of the night, and he was there, sitting at a bench, alone, dressed not in kingly robes, but the lazy and unskilled habit of an ordinary man. He seemed, suddenly, so old and frail and slight, that instead of feeling fear in his presence, she felt … Alys tried to formulate the thought … compassion. Or perhaps it was sorrow, as she would feel for a one magnificent but felled oak tree.

It was then that she was able to reappraise him, to see him as an older man, a father, perhaps even a grandfather. It was an unfamiliar man's office which she'd barely known her entire existence. Her own father, the King of France, had been absent from virtually all of her life. And there sat King Henry of England, feared by every man and beast, supping his meal like an old man sitting upright in bed, seen as only she could see him. Not as a great and regal king, but as an ordinary aging man, grey-haired, somewhat bent of body, spilling some of his pottage from his spoon, and even mumbling to himself.

Where had once been a man of virility and substance, a man around whom others trod warily, now sat a humbled man, like a tethered giant. For old Henry had become a man whose day had passed. And seeing him now and into his future, she felt a wave of immense sadness. Yet when she sat down opposite him and she realised that he was seeing her as a woman for the first time, she saw with unrestrained delight that the fires in his eyes were suddenly lit. She saw desire which was inspired by her, and she saw a man who could be both husband and lover, father and brother, mentor and protector, a man who would look after, and in return, a man whom she could nurture and protect. And over the months of closeness between them, when she grew from child to true woman, as she drew closer and closer to him, as their child blossomed in her belly and was born, she had grown to love him with all her heart. Yes, people whispered in corridors about the vast difference in their ages, but shadow voices were of no consequence, and she paid them no heed. Nor did she care what people thought of her, for the only opinions which mattered about her being the king's mistress, were hers and Henrys.

Yet despite her love for old Henry, while others feared him, while armies were slaughtered by his brilliance as a tactician and commander, while men still died at his command, Alys saw him as a fatherly, lonely and remote man in desperate need of love; not the love of a courtier or son or daughter who depended on his love for their welfare, but a reciprocated love, a heartfelt love of soul for soul, body for body, heart for heart.

He was a man bereft, surrounded by obsequious

courtiers, hated by his family, isolated from all those he thought were friends because of his absolute power, sought out by adventurous women of the court because of the favours he could bestow ... but in truth Princess Alys knew old Henry as an older man who was desperate for the love and affection of a woman. Nor just any women, for as King, he had his choice of women servants and wives and daughters of courtiers upon whom he happened. Any woman was available to the King of England. But it wasn't just a woman he wanted, desired, lusted for, required and needed, but one woman alone; a woman who nurtured him, cared for him, and ordered a bath when he was tired so that she could wash his body, cleanse it, perfume and cherish it, and make it ready for his next stage of his day. And most especially for the decision she prayed that he would make on behalf of herself and their beloved son William.

And as they stood before the fire, even in the warmth of a mild summer evening, they glowed with the heat and their love and the feeling of cleanliness. At this very moment, she could have asked him to gift her the city of Jerusalem, and he would have ridden with a vast army conquer and capture it, simply in order to fulfil her desires.

But now was not the time to ask him about the disposition of his inheritance. Now, at this moment, King Henry the Second of England and Aquitaine was revelling in life itself, in the truth of what a person's life should be. Whether that person in his realms was a king or an Earl, a Yeoman or a peasant, each and every man and woman deserved a life embraced by the love of a partner such as he was now enjoying. It was a life he should have enjoyed in the loving embrace of his Queen Eleanor, and for years he did until ambition turned her from Ruth to Jezebel. Yet because he was omnipotent, he had still enjoyed those times with others than Eleanor. His was, and continued to be a life merited by the courtesies of his mistresses, the once-living Rosamund and now the young and vital Alys.

And as he closed his eyes, sitting in a carver and reflecting upon the joys he'd just experienced in the bath, Alys knew in her heart what was the right time to broach the future life and safety of herself and their son, William. It would be tonight, after she had satisfied his body. She would time her discussion as he was about to fall into a deep and satisfying sleep, now he was bathed and refreshed, and once his body had been drained of its tensions. That was the time, so that hers would be the last words he would hear before the blessed angels carried him gently in their loving embrace into the land of dream. And if God be praised, it would be the thought he would wake up to in the morning, thinking that it was his thought and not hers.

"Yes! Yes to all things, my love. Yes to ridding myself and this realm of those bastards, my sons, who have stabbed me in my back; yes to ridding myself and this nation of my wife who would kill me each day of the week 'till Kingdom Come. Yes to the armies of France and Spain, Portugal and others led by my sons, who will attack me when they see I'm weak, for then I will bring my righteous might to bear down upon them and crush them as I should have twenty years hence.

"But my son John ... he is faithful to me, he is innocent of his brothers' and his mother's lies and deceits, he is but a boy. How can I make him into a bastard? Annulling my marriage to Eleanor will not discriminate between my sons and daughters, good or evil. They will all be cast out and become like dirt beneath the feet of all who tread their path. Yes, all the sons save John deserve no mercy, and also save but my good daughters. All my sons, bar John, are rotten to their very cores ... and yes, I would not hesitate to make bastards of the bastards. They have earned the mantles of dishonour by right of their actions as my children, because of their evil and unnatural behaviour. And my Eleanor ... yes ... she too deserves to have lived her life without me as her sire, annulled, quit and dismissed by not one, but two husbands in the space of a single lifetime.

"But John. Dear God, Alys, how can I cast my John, my Prince, my true-born son into the wilderness, to wander this earth never having had a father, spat upon as a lowly bastard, yet with a father whom he loves and who loves him with a great zeal?" asked King Henry. "The only one of my sons who stands beside me, who came to me when others were conspiring against me ..."

His voice drifted into silence as they sat, alone, in the banqueting hall of Everswell. The servants had been dismissed when they had served the breakfast meal, and Henry had told her that he'd been thinking about their conversation of the previous night, and how it affected him.

"But Henry, my Lord, the welfare of John is dear to my heart as it is to yours. Had he not rejected me as a wife, as your son Richard rejected me, I would have married him and then he could have been co-regent with little William, as you are co-regent with young Henry. Yet when Queen Eleanor suggested me as his bride in order to keep my dowry, John said outright, in my very presence, pointing at me as though I was a village whore, *"I will not dip my manhood where my father has already muddied the pond."* It was a cruel remark, but one for which I was willing to forgive. So as he will not have me as his bride, I will adopt him as my son, and I will protect him as best I can with those who remain loyal to you," she said.

Henry looked at her in surprise. "Loyalty to me dies when I breathe my last breath," he said. "My counsellors, courtiers and dearest friends will lift their eyes from my grave and seek out that king who can best grant them a rich future. But yes, what you say is good. Adopting John will make him your son, despite the similar ages you share. And as a brother to my William, I pray he will come to love him as I love the little lad.

"But that still leaves the intractable nature of young Henry, Richard, Geoffrey and especially Eleanor. Their deaths will be the only security of which you and William can be assured. And that will not happen. Not while I am alive. When I am dead, their fates are in God's hands, but while I am alive, and father and husband, despite their treason against me, they are still and always will be my sons.

"So I am once again left with the same two problems with which my mind has wrestled since our son was born … how to secure your and William's safety after my death, and how to bequeath my lands to young Henry, my heir by right of birth, without Richard and Geoffrey ensuring his demise? No army is capable of beating back young Richard when his temper is flared and his zeal is driven by God-given ambition," said Henry quietly, tearing another lump of bread from the loaf.

"My Liege," she said quietly, even though there was nobody else to hear, yet for her, it increased the secrecy of her plans, "I too have thought of little else since our son was born. We must all face our mortal end, and by virtue of your age, and mine, your end will come sooner than that of your mistress and your son. The only way is for you to annul Eleanor, marry me, disinherit your sons, and allow John to become William's brother. Then I am secure, John becomes secure, William is secure, and your kingdoms here and in France will go to the sons who love you the greatest, and in whom you can have nothing but trust."

"You ask me to disinherit my flesh and blood, Alys. As though it were nothing more than a contract to be rescinded, torn up, nullified. A parchment to be scrapped at will. But these are my boys, and no matter how they treat me, as their father, how can I treat them in a similar vein? I love them, despite what they have done. I think of my Henry, my Richard, my Geoffrey, and even now, my heart swells with pride. I see them ride in front of an army, and I think that England and Aquitaine are secure in their hands. And these are the future of my realms, which I have fought for all my life, yet you ask me to cast them aside; to forgo my heritage as a King of England? Oh Alys, these are my sons, not pieces of parchment," he said sadly. He looked down at the table, and stared into his bowl of pottage. Then he looked up into Alys's eyes, and sighed, "Where is King Solomon when he is so badly needed, my Queen of Sheba?"

Sarum castle, Wiltshire, two weeks later.

Queen Eleanor of England and Aquitaine continued to smile, long after the masque had ended and long after the players had left. It was remarkable how the Seneschal of the Castle somehow managed to snare such good passing troubadours and actors. When she lived as Queen beside her old husband Henry, she was accustomed to the performances of the very best poets, musicians and bards which the nation produced. Some players came from over the sea, which was an additional delight. Yet when she was first confined to her prison in Sarum Castle, she'd anticipated day after day, night after night of a life of vacancy, of no entertainment, no singing, no masques, no banquets in a land bereft of the arts and poetry, music and other culture to which she'd been born. She'd expected old Henry to reward her attempts to dethrone him with a barbarity earned by traitors. And she'd waited for his punishments to be metered out. For a *chasseur* of armed men to arrive in the dead of night, to drag her out in her bedwear, tie her two arms and two legs between four stallions and let them pluck her apart like a roasted chicken in a feast.

But it never happened, and as the days of her interminable imprisonment grew and grew into months and then years, she began to understand that, because of the remnants of his love for her, or his respect for her as his Queen ... or his fear of the repercussions of his actions when they were known to the Kings of other nations ... was treating her as an honoured guest.

Yes, she was separated from her husband and her children, from many of her court, but no woman could have asked for more comfort, and no prisoner could have expected a jail with such gentle bars. Her only restrictions, by order of old Henry, were her movements beyond the grounds of Sarum Castle. She still hunted, fished, rode and walked in freedom, but that freedom was restricted by the boundaries of the land on which Sarum stood, and by the Captain of the fifteen guards who rode and remained with her everywhere.

Her bodily needs were well satisfied by three excellent personal cooks, by bathing once every three weeks, and by a young guardsman, ignorant as a boar but strong as an ox, who satisfied her when her womanly urges began throbbing. Though she was a matron of fifty-five summers, it often surprised her that when she walked past a tall and muscular guard standing in a corridor, her thighs still pulsated with the desires she had experienced first as a young woman.

But despite the silken ropes which constrained her to this windy and miserable castle, despite the comforts which old Henry had ensured she enjoyed, Eleanor still missed the authority she once exercised as Queen of England and Aquitaine, as co-Monarch with Henry when he was away at war, and as the most powerful woman in the world. She yearned for her freedom as earnestly as a nun yearned to be visited at night by Christ. She communicated in secret with all of her sons, save John. She wrote to, but had yet to enjoy a response from the Kings of France and Spain, Portugal, and the Kingdoms of Italy. The Pope had sent her a letter which should have been delivered by a Bishop, but he was forbidden to enter her presence. It was a letter wishing her good fortune, to put her trust in the word of the Lord, and the Pope begged her to pray for Henry's forgiveness, so that her dignity could be restored. She'd torn it up in abject fury and sent the pieces into the fire. Even a year later, and to this day, she cursed the name of Pope Alexander III, both for ignoring her pleas for assistance, and for daring to defy her husband Henry and cite his Papal authority over that of a King.

It was only at Christmas that she was freed during the holiday season. The time of the birth of the Saviour, the time of merriment and joy at the first coming of the Kingdom of Heaven on Earth, the time when old Henry relented his strict prohibitions, and allowed his family to gather. Not to be a loving family, but to establish control, to lance festering sores, to attempt, foolishly, to make some sort of peace.

They met sometimes in Aquitaine, sometimes in Windsor, sometimes in London. It was only six months before she would see him and her children again, and she revelled in the thought of sitting with them as a family, hearing their stories of their exploits, delighting in their grasps of life. Yes, there would be vicious quarrels, threats, swords and knives drawn; but Eleanor knew that while anger would fill the air, beneath and beyond that, there was a love which she knew old Henry felt for her and her children, and which, somehow, they felt for both her as their mother and him as their father.

And despite her anger at him, she knew in the very depths of her heart that one day, perhaps next year or in a year after, some sort of sense would prevail and he would reconcile with his children, return her to her rightful throne as the wife of the King of England, and things would return to what had once been a semblance of normality.

And Queen Eleanor continued to believe that, until the arrival of the Baroness Maud, the goodwife of the Baron Turstin FitzRolf. Eleanor had known Maud for twenty-five years, yet was still surprised when late one afternoon, out of the lands towards the east of Sarum, a small group of riders accompanied by six lancers, paced towards her castle.

She saw them from a battlement facing towards distant Windsor and London, and at first, peered to see who it could be. As they rode over a distant hill and came closer, Eleanor saw that there was a tent over the middle horse's rider, and so Eleanor couldn't make out the identity, but to assemble such a *chasseur* would mean that the person must be of considerable wealth, almost certainly a courtier. But why would a courtier visit the Queen when it had been expressly forbidden by old King Henry?

As they drew nearer, the assembly suddenly pulled to a halt, and two of the guardsmen dismounted, and removed the tent covering the rider. To her surprise, Eleanor saw, even in the fading light, that it was a woman. A woman dressed in considerable finery. A maid who accompanied her also dismounted, and spent several moments on a ladder propped up beside the woman's horse, arranging her headwear, her collars and her dress. Then the group remounted, and at a slower pace, stepped towards the Castle. To Queen Eleanor's shock and surprise, it was Maud, wife of the Baron FitzRolf, who was a dear friend. Yet her husband, Turstin was her enemy; he was as close as any man to old King Henry, and would support the monarch regardless of the rights or wrongs of the situation.

So Maud had sided with her husband, and had come to do Eleanor harm, she thought. Suddenly angry, Eleanor stormed off the battlements, down the circular stone steps of the Keep to the lower floors of her castle and waited for Baroness Maud to be admitted and introduced. Should she keep her waiting a day, or maybe two, in order to teach her not to follow the plan which she was so clearly following this day? No, Eleanor was anxious for news of the goings-on in London or Windsor or wherever Henry was, and any information was gratefully and willingly received. The tension of waiting until tomorrow or the next day would make her head explode.

Within half of the hour, when the sun had already sunk beneath the western hills, Eleanor was sitting in her privy chambers, surrounded by maidservants, when there was a knock on her door. The Seneschal of the Castle appeared, and announced that Her Grace, the Baroness Maud FitzRolf, had arrived, and sought an appointment with her Majesty.

"Maud?" said Eleanor in surprise. "Maud FitzRolf is here? In Sarum? Send the Lady in."

Maud entered with a flourish of skirts and bowed low to her Queen. Then she stood, and approached Eleanor to kiss the ring on her hand.

"Sit, my dear old friend. How wonderful to see you. And how magnificent you look. Were you passing on your way to ... to ... somewhere, or have you come to see me?" asked Eleanor, trying to sound innocuous.

"Majesty, at considerable danger to me, and without my husband's knowledge and consent, I have come to see you," she said.

One of Eleanor's maids brought her over a goblet, and from a carafe, poured wine. Then she offered her cake, which Maud greedily ate, the ride having given her a hunger which was penetrating her being.

Frowning, Eleanor asked, "But why risk your own and your beloved husband's lives in order to visit your wrongfully-imprisoned queen?"

"Majesty, there is much to tell you, much you should know, and more even to think about. But the time to tell is for later. For now, I wish to ask after your health and welfare. I know, and can see, that King Henry treats you like no other prisoner, but ..."

"Baroness Maud. We have been friends for many, many years. You've attended my confinements, travelled with me throughout my realms, feasted and churched with me when the time required it. You have been much more to me than a sister. If you have something to tell me, something which I should know, then I need and want to hear it immediately," said Eleanor, leaving Maud in no doubt as to what to say next.

Her visitor nodded, sipped another draft of the ale, and said softly, "Madam, you must be aware of the relationship of your Henry with the strumpet, the whore of France, Alys."

"Of course. And I don't blame the child. While I blamed and cursed Fair Rosamund for her seduction of my husband, Alys was but a child when he took her, and I am devoid of hatred towards the young Princess because of the difference in their ages and the power between them," said Eleanor. "She has never had a true father nor a mother, and though God knows it's against Nature, she looked upon Henry as father, husband, lover and protector, and I am unwilling to blame her ... Henry, yes, he I curse for his seduction of a child, but not sweet little Alys, a child in all but body," said Eleanor.

Maud nodded. "A testament to your goodness, Highness. But you are doubtless aware that in the past year, she has had a child with your husband, one William. A bastard. Yet a bastard who remains with his mother ... and his father Henry."

"Of course. I may be imprisoned, but voices come to

me over the battlements," said Eleanor.

Now Maud remained silent, not knowing how to progress with her narration. She had been trying to find the right words, to phrase her information in such a way that the Queen's legendary temper didn't suddenly erupt, as was the way of the Devil's Brood, and injure the story-teller.

"Majesty ... Eleanor ... my husband, to his eternal shame and condemnation, has suggested a plan to his Majesty, King Henry, a plan conceived in the festering bogs of Hell, something which I abhor ... a plan which concerns the future of the Angevin dynasty ... of your sons ... of ... of ... oh Dear God in Heaven ... of you, Eleanor."

The Queen looked at the Baroness and frowned. What in God's name was she talking about? One minute she was talking about Princess Alys, a silly child who had filled the eye of old Henry, but would be gone when the apple rotted on the bough, and the next minute, she was saying ...

... and then a terrible realisation dawned on Queen Eleanor. It was something which she hadn't considered in a dozen years, not since she'd been confined in a silken prison. Her husband could have had her pulled limb from limb by stallions, yet while she lived and thrived, the horror of those early thoughts had dissipated like a morning mist over a pond. Those thoughts were something which the months and months of isolation had enabled her to totally discount. But now that his little bastard William had become the talk of the court, now that he was keeping him by his side, both the bastard and her son, John Lackland ... now that Henry's new son and her Prince John were players in the game of kings, it had suddenly become a reality once again.

As the realisation of what the Baroness was saying dawned on Eleanor's mind, her mouth opened as though she was about to espouse an idea ... and then closed. Then she opened her mouth again, stood up from her chair, braced herself from fainting, and at the top of her lungs, screamed out, "WHAT? Is this some madman's tale, like Floris and Blancheflour? My husband, my Henry will ... he's going to annul me? ANNUL ME ....!!!! Eleanor???? *Daemonus Henricus est Deus Inversus ... Fortuna Imperatrix Mundi!* Dear God Almighty in His Heaven, the Wheel of Fortune spins in opposition to me!"

Suddenly terrified of the vision of insanity before her, Baroness Maud sank back into her chair in horror and fear.

But Queen Eleanor wasn't looking or thinking of her. She stared out into the space of the room, and screamed, "I will end that man forever. I will cut his body into a thousand pieces and let the dogs devour him. Like Medea, I will cut up William and serve him as stew to Henry and his whore Alys. God help me, but I will!!"

She sat down, and withdrew into herself, muttering and mumbling, as though the Baroness was absent, and Eleanor was alone in the room.

Maud didn't know whether to stand silently and leave her, or to sit there and wait for the legendary temper to pass.

That night, the Baroness dined with Eleanor, but the meal was uncomfortable. Long periods of silence were interrupted by sharp and deliberate questions from Eleanor about who in the court continued to support old Henry, who now gave fealty to the whore Alys, who was taking a command of the affairs of state when old Henry and his whore were abed in Woodstock?

Citing a headache from the length of the journey, the Baroness excused herself at one hour to midnight, and took herself to bed.

By the following morning, even before Eleanor had risen, she, her maids and her chasseurs had left the castle and ridden off westwards in the direction of London. Not that Queen Eleanor was surprised or disappointed. Now that she was informed of a threat against her status, and especially that of her sons, she had a great deal of work to do and being hostess to a visitor would delay her on her path forward.

Smuggling letters out of the castle was always difficult. The Seneschal and the Chief of her Guard were scrupulous in their loyalty to old King Henry, and searched every pocket, every bag and every crevice of a man- or maid-servant whom Eleanor sent out from the castle for a special purpose. Several times, she had played with the guards, and hidden a special message in the bodice of one of her maids, but when the chief guard had brought it back to her, and placed it back on the table before her in a moment of triumph, she broke the seal, opened it, showed it to him, and explained that it was merely an instruction to the victualler of Salisbury to provide her maid with fresh honey.

But her real way of transmitting messages was at night, unknown to the guards or the Seneschal. It was by message-bearing pigeon. Though a dove was first used by Noah in the Bible, pigeons were growing in use as ways of sending messages between distant peoples. Queen Eleanor took the idea from one of the gardeners, who bred and trained pigeons, both as messengers and for sport. For a purse full of gold, he agreed to train one of his pigeons. One day, he absented himself, citing a sudden fever, and took his pigeon in a cage all the way to Windsor castle, where he paid a guard to release the bird the following morning. In that way, the bird quickly learned the route from the King's castle to Eleanor's prison.

From that time, the clever pigeon had taken messages between Eleanor and Prince Richard in Windsor, who then gave the information to young Henry and Geoffrey. So long as she crept up to the battlements in the black of the night and released the bird when the guards were looking elsewhere, nobody saw a lone pigeon fly from the castle westwards.

And a day later, when the pigeon returned carrying a message from her sons, it landed on a battlement, and she managed to secrete herself so that the bird hopped down and into a little cage which the gardener had created for her. Reaching in and taking the tied parchment from its leg was a simple task.

Angry that none of her sons had warned her of what she'd recently learned from the Baroness Maud, she forgave them, as she knew they were still doing penance.

She knew that their movements were constrained, and they were watched every hour of the day.

But what was now urgent was to instil in them a feeling of greater dread for their futures and their inheritance, than their fear of offending their father. She had to provoke them to rise up, yet again, to arm themselves, to defend themselves, and to persuade other kings to give them armies, so that once and for all time, Henry could be expunged from this world, and she and her children would be the rightful heirs of his kingdoms.

And all depended on her doing it swiftly, because by her calculations, the time to act would be when old Henry brought all his family together at Aquitaine for the Christmas festivities.

Windsor Castle west of London November 1177

For some moments during the past several months, Princess Alys had breathed a sigh of relief, and found some ease in her situation. During those moments, she could breathe in without her breath catching in her throat; she could look out at the country in which her castle was situated, and appreciate the scudding clouds, the warmth of the sun on her body, the chirping of crickets and the buzz of flies. On these occasions when she was like her former self, young, full of hope for her future and grasping her life as best she could. On these occasions, old Henry talked openly, willingly, about his coming divorce from Eleanor, and the disinheritance of his sons.

But like taffeta rubbed against the nap, he changed from light to dark, and then the talk was of how to defend her and his beloved William against Henry, Richard and Geoffrey when he died. He knew, of course, that his queen was the real problem facing Alys and William after his death, but rarely did he talk about Eleanor, because when he did, his stomach ached, and he had to take a potion to calm down the snakes writhing in his belly.

Only occasionally did Alys join his discussions, because now that she had made her plans known, now that her King was familiar with them, what had become important was to allow her old Henry to work out for himself how to achieve her goals. In his old age, he had become increasingly irritable with courtiers and servants, yet there was not a moment's discord between them, not with her or their William, who were a constant source of safety, security, peace and harmony.

But the space between his good self and his irritable

self was covered by little more than a flimsy curtain, and she was loathe to risk ruffling it by stressing the urgency of his decision. He knew, as well as she, that the path to her safety led to the annulment of Eleanor and the dismissal of the then-bastard sons by her. For Alys, the road ahead was simple, but she knew from the way in which her old Henry agonised over every potential fork in the road, that all roads ahead were strewn with sharp boulders.

Only he, and he alone, could determine which road he would take. She had guided him to a place where he could step down her path, but he could just as easily turn around, abandon Alys and their William, and return to the path of his existing family. The imaginary signposts she had erected to guide his thoughts, but to do more than that, were intended to lead his horse down her road, but she was all too aware that the slightest wrong move could have devastating consequences for her. And so she must temper her impatience and fear with caution, love, hope and comfort, and allow his mind to determine her future.

It was one morning, over the breakfast meal, after a gentle and loving night of comfort and bodily ease, that he said to her, "Christmas."

That was all. A single word which she had to interpret.

"My liege? Christmas?"

"Aquitaine. Christmas at Aquitaine," he said, dipping a lump of bread into a vat of honey. "We will spend this Christmas at Aquitaine."

"Excellent," she said, waiting for him to continue with his thoughts.

"I will instruct my court of my desires. I will only take a few of my courtiers. But my sons ... all of my sons ... will join me, as will my wife Queen Eleanor. I allow her some freedom for the Christmas festivities before I return her to her prison. It's good for her blood, and it frees her soul, even though for just a few weeks."

Alys was suddenly obsessed by an intense fear. It gripped her throat and she found it difficult to breathe. "The Queen? Eleanor? At Aquitaine? With Richard? With Henry? With ..."

"She comes each year, as do my boys," said Henry, failing to see the fear in his lover's face. "It's like uncorking a bottle of wine and letting the noxious fumes escape. It stops her from mouldering."

"So William and I will not be joining you, Sire," she said softly.

He looked at her in amazement. "Of course you will.

We have to resolve the situation of my realms after my death, just so that I can go to my Maker with a peaceful mind. And meeting all of us at Christmastime is the best way. I've thought of little else these past few months. Only by bringing all the actors into the same theatre, can the play be resolved. Yes, there will be shouting and screaming, curses and threats; but that's the Angevin family for you. The Devil's Brood. But it's all piss and wind. Much is said, little is meant. Much mud is thrown, little sticks to the walls. Yet by having you and William, Eleanor and myself, as well as my Henry, Richard, Geoffrey and John, all of us in the same halls, we will reach a resolution. One which will be happy for you, for me, and which I pray won't lead to another armed uprising by my turbulent sons."

"Not all will be happy, Sire," she said softly.

"True," said Henry, "until I release her forever and put her back onto her throne, Eleanor will never be happy. Whatever I do, dealing with my sons or with you and William, she will always be plotting and scheming behind my back. Why the very thought of her being in my presence makes my shoulders ache, for that's where she'll stab the knife.

"You see, Alys, the very act of dividing land for

inheritance has plagued kings since the time of Solomon. Though ours is, and if providence by my guide, will be one of the greatest dynasties mankind has ever known, we are, as a family, no different from every other royalty. If young Henry takes it all, as is his right by primogenitor, then what of Richard and Geoffrey? John has made his bed with me, but my death will expose the poor lad. So as to my other sons, will they sit on their arses and allow their brother Henry to prevail, or will they wait until my funeral ends before striking at him. Will John's young body be found floating in the Thames, or will I be able to reach a satisfactory resolution whereby I can die in peace?"

"And if John takes all of my kingdoms as co-regent with our William, what of Eleanor and Henry, of Richard and Geoffrey? My daughters will marry kings, and so they aren't my problem. But my sons? That's why I have to sit them before me, their father, husband and king, and inform them of my decisions."

Suddenly shocked to hear that word, one she'd waited for him to say for months, she asked cautiously, "Decisions? Has your majesty made a decision?"

"None so far, dearest. My heart tells me to annul Eleanor and disinherit these traitorous bastards. Boys I nurtured, brought them to manhood, boys to whom I once gave my heart, but now, as men, they would see me dead beside a road and laugh as my body was torn to pieces by foxes and dogs. No decision yet. My head tells me that the moment I announce what is my intention, I'm placing your life in dire jeopardy. It would be like placing you, holding little William, on the top of a castle battlement in a howling wind, and praying you won't fall. Yet I know my kin, and it's certain that when they see you, alone and teetering on a tower, Eleanor and my sons will scream up at you to dash yourselves on the rocks below. So when comes Christmastime, by then I will have decided, and I will make my decision known. So long as I'm there, I can remain in control, and can save you and him."

"But from what you say, Henry, nothing can save me. Name me Queen and call our William King jointly with your John, and when you die, we will be attacked by the legions of the damned. Young Henry, Richard and Geoffrey will raise armies from France, Spain, Italy and Portugal, and fall on England like the hounds of hell. All following Queen Eleanor, riding behind the avenging Angel Gabriel. Yes, we have an English army loyal to you, but on your death, where will their loyalty lie? With me? With baby William? With John, aged not eleven and in his minority? Surely they will turn and kneel to their new king, one who can lead them into battle."

"Not if you're my Queen by marriage! Not if John and William are my successors! Not if I name as regent the Baron Turstin FitzRolf until John, and then William reach their majority. Until they are old enough to lead an army," he said.

But she could tell by listening to his tone, that his mouth might be speaking, but his heart was silent.

Poitiers castle Aquitaine, central France.
Four days before Christmas, December 1177

The weather was freezing cold, and presaged snow, despite the sky being coloured a light blue. Only an occasional cloud marred the attempt of the anaemic winter sun to warm the lands and the waters of Poitiers Castle. Old Henry, wrapped in the fur of a bear, yet shivering in the frigid atmosphere of the late afternoon, stood high on the battlements, looking down on the Loire River in the direction of the distant sea. He knew that it would be at least two days before Eleanor's arrival, but his knotted stomach, and the constant quarrelling of his sons, drove him to seek the solitude of the castle heights.

Perhaps her boat would sink and she would drown, which would end some of his problems; perhaps a sudden wave would erupt from the depths and sweep her overboard so that the last thing anyone heard of her was Eleanor calling out for help; or perhaps a sudden storm would send a lightning bolt from the heavens and suffuse her with St. Elmo's Fire before she jumped screaming into the water to quench the glow.

Perhaps all those things would happen, for they were certainly happening in his mind. Yet for all that, for all his desire to see her dead, dismissed and gone forever, he yearned to see her. He loved Alys with all his heart, just as he had loved Rosamund ... yet in all the world, in all of history, there had only, ever, been one Eleanor of Aquitaine. Proud, strong, beautiful, brilliant, the most magnificent of all magnificent women, in equal measure as fierce in her love as she was fervent in her hatred. He feared and loved her, admired and loathed her. She was the wall which stopped his progress, yet the gateway to his joy. When first he'd seen her as a youth of nineteen, he could barely speak he was so overwhelmed. Lust? Love? Desire? Yes, all these emotions, and more. But today, after a lifetime of deep and abiding love mixed with a lifetime of unrequited anger and distrust, he waited for her appearance like a miscreant boy waiting before his master for the punishment of a wrong-doing. To his surprise, he realised he was smiling, not in anticipation of her arrival, but because of the irony of his situation. He, Henry of England and Aquitaine, was the most powerful man in the world, yet in the depths of his being, he knew that it was to Eleanor, weak and imprisoned and powerless, to whom the Goddess Fortuna had given her Sword of Destiny.

And for reasons he couldn't fathom, it was at times like this, at a time when his sons were being their most evil and burdensome selves, that he missed Eleanor the most. Despite their constant disputes, only Eleanor could calm the animals his sons became when the entire family was together. All he could do was to shout, threaten and draw a sword, yet with one momentary stare, with one arched eyebrow, Eleanor could calm Richard, force Henry to apologise, and make Geoffrey withdraw.

Having dismissed his servants and courtiers, and alone on the battlements except for the guards standing to attention at each end of the parapet, he breathed in and out as deeply as he could, if for no other reason than to expel the noxious air which filled the castle when his sons were venting their fury. He knew that there would be anger and arguments, but he hadn't expected it to begin as Richard stepped off the boat and into the Castle.

The previous night, within an hour of their arrival, Henry had forbidden them to speak, but their silence was more thunderous than their arguments. He'd sent them to other parts of the castle, but despite his being alone with Alys and William, he swore that he could hear them shouting, complaining ... breathing.

Bringing Alys and William had been a mistake. A well-intentioned, but very real mistake. His lover, mistress and companion had been correct. Though but a girl in the eyes of the world, she held a wisdom which would have made a philosopher envious. He thought that when his boys saw his love for her and his little son, they might be pleased for their father, sufficient to accept her as his mistress and love.

But Alys had warned that him that she and William would be like oil poured on a flame, and she had been right.

When the lads arrived at the dock on the river under heavily armed escort, they had been welcomed by old Henry and had greeted him with deference and courtesy. But the moment that they entered the Castle's privy rooms, and saw Alys and her bastard, their step-brother William, sitting like a loving family before a roaring fire, their moods changed from respect to unquenchable hostility.

Richard's lips actually snarled, and he spat, "What's that woman doing here? Why is she at our family Christmas gathering?"

Before Henry could speak, Alys stood from before the fire, and smiled, "And I bid you all the greetings of this joyous season, Princes Richard, Henry and Geoffrey. I welcome you to Poitiers."

"It is not your place to say these things, Alys. I need no welcome from you, Madam, to my home. My home. Not yours. Now or ever," he sneered.

"My home!" roared old King Henry, his temper suddenly flaring at the insult to his woman. "My home, Sir, by my marriage to your mother, by her dowry, by her years as my queen. My home, Richard ... MY castle. And if I choose to invite my Lady Alys and my son William as my guests, then take note, Sir, that it is my choice. You have neither say nor volition. Since raising an army against me, you are as nothing in my eyes, and if you wish to climb the steep walls back into my favour, you will accord respect to Alys and William."

"Death would be a preference before paying such an accord to a whore who has seduced my father, and to the bastard who has resulted," he said.

Suddenly furious, old Henry screamed a strangled cry, and stepped forward drawing his sword. Richard took an immediate defensive position, drawing his sword, and holding it aloft, ready to parry his father's weapon aside, and then swing his around to bring it crashing down onto old Henry's naked head. Alys screamed in fear of what could suddenly happen to the two men, but her scream made old Henry stop in his tracks, and lower his weapon. Then he said, "Death, Sir, is your preference. And I have ten dozen men who will accommodate your desire for death should I say the word.

Suddenly, young Henry intervened, "Family ... father, brother ... Princess Alys and your little son ... is this the way to begin the Christmas festivities? We are brought here to celebrate the birth of the Saviour, Christ the Redeemer. Yet we begin our visit with calumny, quarrel, and threats? Please, let us stay calm, and remember the love which should be the bedrock of every family."

"Love?" hissed Richard. "Love between husband and wife yes! But love between a man and his one penny whore? And worse, the unnatural love between our old father Samson and his Delilah, a girl I rejected, a lover young enough to be his daughter!"

"Shut your mouth, boy," shouted old Henry. "How will you speak when I have your malevolent tongue cut out?"

"And how will you do it, Father, if I've just run you through with my sword. For you know I can empale you before you have a chance to call for your guards. Then, by your death and his right as your eldest, my brother Henry will be king, Geoffrey and I will become Dukes of our own lands, and God help those once loved by you but unloved by your sons who are left behind," said Richard. "For God alone knows that we will show them no mercy."

But that was too much, even for his brothers. As one, young Henry and Geoffrey shouted, "Richard ... silence ... enough!"

Ignoring them, Richard continued to shout, "Do you think that our mother hasn't already warned us of what you intend to do, Father? You and the whore who now bears your children? Do you really think that we're in ignorance of your plans to dispose of us as though we were rancid meat? To quit your wife and cast her into the darkness? Do you think we know nothing of how you scheme and connive with this witch to whom you've given your aging body?"

At the increase in shouting in the room, little William began to cry in fear of his safety. The old King looked over to where his love, Alys, stood bereft and alone and his babe William lay on a rug. He was suddenly furious, but glancing at Alys and knowing he must not fight his son, he shouted, "You know my plans? You, boy! So headstrong you don't even know whether it's morn or night. How do you know my plans when I myself don't know them yet?"

Richard smiled. "A little bird told me, Father. A bird flew in through my window and told me."

Terrified that the impetuous Richard would give away their mother's secret way of writing to them, young Henry shouted, "Richard! As your Liege Lord, I command you to be silent. Immediately. Not another word, Sir."

At which, the impetuous young Prince, knowing that he shouldn't have mentioned any hint of his mother's pigeons, turned on his heels, stormed out and hadn't been seen until the next day.

And in some ways, old Henry was pleased that Richard was not participating in the family celebrations until Eleanor arrived. He was taking his food in his apartments, riding with a small guard into the nearby forests to hunt boar, and doubtless having whores delivered at night from the nearby town.

All that had happened in the previous few days. He hadn't seen Richard since, and had barely set eyes on young Henry or Geoffrey, other than in the banqueting hall to take food for themselves and retire to their apartments. In a way, he was glad, for when the fight came, as surely it would tomorrow, it would be on the arrival of Eleanor and the unleashing of such a convocation of demons, that he didn't know whether he had the strength still to oppose them all.

He shivered. Suddenly overcome with the cold, Henry walked unsteadily along the parapet and warmed himself at the brazier beside the sentry.

"How do you not freeze up here?" he asked.

The sentry smiled, and said, "By your leave, Highness, when you and your family are down below, I hug this fire as though it was my wife. So long as there is wood to make my flames, I can bear it. But it's as cold as a witch's tits up here when the sun goes down, so this isn't my favourite duty. What I like is kitchen duty. Warmth, food, drink, all at your expense, Sire."

Old Henry laughed, wished the guard good fortune, and then descended into the family apartments two floors below. And the scene which greeted him warmed his very being. Alys was lying on the rugs before the fire, with little William balancing on her stomach gripped safely in her hands; and she was quietly singing him a song and he was making noises to try to emulate her cadences.

She didn't notice Henry's arrival as he stood at the doorway for long moments, just looking at the scene of love, of tranquillity and of tenderness. His heart melted as her love for their child, her innocence, and her utter lack of guile, seemed to spread throughout the room and engulf him. Why couldn't his other family be like young Alys? Why did his sons, save for John, have to grow into monsters, and not remain innocent and guiltless like William? Why was he incapable of bringing love and harmony into the lives of Eleanor and her brood? What was it that made young Alys ... and indeed the late, beloved and greatly-missed Rosamund ... so different from his lawful querulous family to whom the capricious but Almighty God had given all rights and consent? Why should such a devoted, loving and amiable young woman and her son not have the right to inherit what he'd spent an entire lifetime building, especially when his sons looked on his possessions like feral cats fighting over a fatted calf?

But life wasn't that simple, especially for a King ...

for a Plantagenet king and for the great-grandson of William the Conqueror! Even in a family room, there was a snakepit with writhing vipers between him and Alys. Yet he had to secure his standing in the eyes of the world by bequeathing his kingdoms to those who would rightly rule when he was mouldering in his grave. And looking at young Alys, at little William, he knew with awful certainty that their lives would immediately be forfeit if he named either as his successors. Yet how could he not? In these moments of solitude, when he wasn't bothered by courtiers or the affairs of state, he could actually see his life in the landscape he had created. And it was at these moments that he realised how much he detested his sons. He didn't hate John, of course, but despite trying and offering him every opportunity, he found it difficult to love the boy.

But his older sons? Where had his love for them gone? Was it by their actions, or his growing contempt for their greed? And that ... their greed ... was the harbinger of doom for the two beautiful young people on the rug in front of the fire. For when he died, he could find no way of saving Alys and his William. They were doomed. It was a harsh and awful thought, but one which continued to grow in his mind as he grew closer in love to Alys and William.

He had loved his sons when they were born, when they teetered on chubby legs around the castle, when they grew hairs and became young men, grasping all that their lives had to offer. He vested all his hopes in them, revelled in their growing skills as youths and then youngsters. But as his love for Eleanor fractured, as her jealousy and anger grew, as his boys began to demand more and more of his lands and heritage than he was willing to cede while he was alive, and when they went off to fight their own battles, he grew increasingly distant from them, and found more and more to criticise in their behaviour.

Eleanor, of course, was the cause of most of the discontent in his family. Had the normal course of kingship been allowed to progress, his sons would have inherited all in God's good time; but she was willing to give the Almighty less and less time to settle the family affairs as her power in the kingdom was gradually taken from her. And as it lessened, the Queen became more and more insistent on her sons' acquiring kingly rights before their due course.

Old King Henry had grown increasingly intransigent and began to view his sons more dispassionately. Though once he loved them with all his heart, now he saw them as jealous, avaricious, presumptuous, and grasping. And for the good of his realms, for his place in the pageant of kings, he couldn't and wouldn't allow them to gain advantage of what he had fought for all his life. Not at their youthful ages; not with Eleanor as their controlling mother, not to the disadvantage of his Alys and William whom he now loved with all his might ... and especially not without a fight!

Yet ... yet how could he disinherit his sons? How could he disturb God's order of precedence? How could he disrupt Nature's way of progressing from generation to generation? How could he annul Eleanor and cede all to John and William? To do so would be to sign a parchment guaranteeing the deaths of Alys and William and most probably John. To do so would be to ensure that when he died, England would be attacked by three armies, all raised by Henry, Richard and Geoffrey in concert with the eager and malevolent Kings of the continent. And in his sons' anger and avarice, did they really, truly, believe that just because they led an army given to them by some king of France or Germany or Spain, that the moment they had gained a victory, the foreign king would merely pack his tent and return home? Of course not. Once foreign armies were victorious on English soil, they would remain and conquer the entire island. How many Anglo-Saxon kings were still alive since William the Conqueror had cut down their dynasty? Where was Edward the Confessor? Where was Athelstan and Aethelred and Aethelwulf? Their reigns had been cut to shreds once the Normans landed and swept through the country like a plague. Dead. All dead.

And didn't his sons realise that by raising a foreign army to fight on English soil, precisely the same thing would happen as it did in 1066? For then England and Wales, Scotland and even Ireland would be gone forever, to become a province of France or Germany or, God forfend, of Spain.

His problems were insuperable and with the imminent arrival of his wife Eleanor, the problems he was facing would become infinitely worse. When his Queen Bee was in the hive, it wasn't honey which would be made, but a concoction which she had been fermenting in her prison in England, one which she'd bring into the Castle, a witch's brew, a hell-broth of snake's venom and rat's piss. And he shuddered again, not in cold this time, but in fear.

In bed, that night, lying beside his beloved Alys, having just enjoyed the comforts of each other's bodies in which they revelled most nights, Henry lay back and tried to rid his mind of the thousands of insistent thoughts which plagued him. She could tell that he wasn't asleep, both by his breathing, and by the occasional and involuntary twitching in his hands and legs.

"My Liege?" she asked softly.

Realising that he was stopping her from sleeping, he snored to convince her that he was actually asleep, but she continued, "Henry, don't pretend. I know when you're sleeping and when you're not. What's troubling you, my love? Was it the quarrel with Richard? That was days ago. Is it the imminent arrival of Queen Eleanor? Is it my presence here in Aquitaine? Tell me and I'll ease your problems."

"Dearest girl," he said, "if you could ease my problems, you would have Solomon's wisdom; yet for all that, everybody would call you the Witch of Endor. I have a hundred problems and not a single solution. For more than a year, since we first became lovers, since my beloved William was born, I have wracked my mind to find a way out of the natural fluxion to which my kingdom is heir, but now that Eleanor is about to descend on Poitiers, now that Richard has staked his claim as the most unworthy son in Christendom, and now that Henry and Geoffrey are sitting atop a casement window like vultures, waiting to pick the flesh of the dead, I fear for your lives more deeply than I have ever done before."

"Then make me your Queen. Pay the Pope, annul Eleanor, make your unworthy sons into bastards, name John and William as co-Regents, and have done with it. Raise an army from your Barons by promising them whatever rewards, and when young Henry and Richard and Geoffrey are beaten, exile them to a far-off land. Call a Crusade and send them off to Jerusalem. Have them spend their strength fighting the accursed Moors. Dear God, Henry, my own father, King Louis of France, launched a crusade thirty years ago when Edessa fell to the Turkman, Zengi. He and King Conrad of Germany petitioned Pope Eugene and set off with your wife, Eleanor."

"Yes," interrupted Henry, "and hundreds of good men were killed, both armies were destroyed by the Seljuks, and your father ... and Eleanor ... just managed to save themselves by reaching Jerusalem."

"Precisely, Henry," she said, soothing his grey hair, "and whatever God wills, then Richard and Henry and Geoffrey will receive. Please God they survive, but their absence will give my son William time to grow, and John will no longer be *Johan sans Terre* but co-ruler of

England and Wales, now Ireland, and soon Scotland. By the time they return, Majesty, England will have a great ruler in John, a future ruler in William, and your heritage is secure for all time."

He sighed. "Oh love, if only it were that simple. Why would my God-forsaken sons go on Crusade when I have just made them bastards? They will stay in England, or worse, go to France and Italy and Spain, and raise an army to cut off my arms and legs before they even consider cutting off my head. Then God help England, because a limbless, headless trunk of a monarch cannot help anybody, least of all the woman and child he loves with all his heart."

She fought back a cry of despair. These were words she'd been dreading to hear, and now she was hearing them. Now that Richard and the other sons were together with her and William, with old Henry and soon with Eleanor, Alys knew in her heart of hearts that her lover's life was about to devolve and sink into a cesspit full of festering Plantagenet hatreds and jealousies, lusts and lifelong animosities, and that she would be dragged down with him.

Now she knew for certain that there was no longer safety in old Henry, nor would her plans ever come to fruition. Her ideas, supported by the Baron FitzRolf had all made sense until a moment ago, when Henry's mind became clear as to his path ahead. For no matter how much he desired it, that path wouldn't include her or her son William.

She thought deeply and allowed her mind to contemplate different scenarios. But each time, it came back to one possibility, and one only. She had to flee. With William. Before old Henry died.

While ever he was alive, she would be spared. But how long could a man of forty-four years continue to live, especially a grey beard who had spent so much of his life in battle, whose body was overfed and now underused other than in the bedroom, a man who lived on his wits and spent more time shouting at courtiers than singing in Church?

And what if he was to be feasting with his friends, and eat and drink too much? What if, like his grandfather Henry the First, he was to die from overeating lampreys? Or what if Richard really had brought his sword down on Henry's neck and delivered a deadly blow? What then of Alys and her son William? Who would care for her, protect her, ensure her survival?

Nobody! Which is why all of the roads her mind

wandered in order to save herself and her little son, William, led to the same destination. To leave this Court, to leave England, and to return to ... to go to ... to journey to ... to seek residency at ...

Which is where her mind came to a stop. For her father, the King of France, would never accept her back, now that she was unwed, yet tainted with the English seed; Italy would never accept her because of the fortune paid every year by the English crown in annates to the Holy See; Spain and Portugal, Germany and Denmark, Sweden and Norway ... none would accept her presence, because to do so would alienate the English monarch, and in young Henry's and Richard's moods, it would lead to war.

She was like a craft on the high seas, full of sail, riding high over the waves, yet without a wheelman and crew, sailing directionless at the behest of wind and tide, seeking a safe harbour. And she knew precisely what happened to those kinds of craft ... they foundered on sharp rocks.

Well, her ship was not going to be sunk. And neither was that of her beloved son. Alys determined, lying in bed beside her lover, that she would be the captain, crew and wheelman of her ship, and she would sail it with her son into a calm, safe port.

She listened to Henry's breathing and realised that this time, he was truly asleep. Despite the love she knew he felt for her and William, there was nothing he could do to save her. And so as of today, as of this moment in time, it was up to her to set a direction for a safe harbour for her and her son. Princesses were supposed to be compliant, to meekly accept the fate they were allowed by their fathers and then their husbands.

But Alys knew at this very moment that she could not rely on Henry. Nor her father Louis, whom she hadn't seen in years and who was as distant from her as any stranger from the North of England. Nor could she rely on the Pope in Rome. Nor any king or queen, prince or nobleman. She could only depend upon herself. The Princess Alys and her son William. Because no matter what happened tomorrow or on Christmas day or in the weeks to follow, either to Henry or his sons, or Eleanor of any member of their family, Alys was now certain that there was no room in this place for her.

Poitiers castle Aquitaine, central France the day before Christmas, December 1177

Only God knew how he knew, but he knew. There had

been no warning, no messenger, no galloping hooves, no feet running in fear and anticipation. How could there be, when she was arriving by horse, and then had to be rowed across from the opposite bank of the wide Loire River. Yet as she drew nearer and nearer, though she was still on the road between Paris where Castle Poitiers of Aquitaine was situated in the region Vienne, the very atmosphere itself seemed to change, as though God Himself was preparing to deliver an apocalyptic storm of torrential rain, shattering thunder and murderous lightening.

But old Henry knew. As he and his sons and daughters, Alys and William, all save still-angry and surly Richard, gathered on the day before Christmas in the Banqueting Hall, Henry suddenly looked up from the table with a pained expression. Concerned, Alys sitting beside him asked how he was feeling. He told her that he was suffering a sudden twinge in his shoulders and ache in his back, and that it would soon go with the relief of a goblet of wine.

It didn't go, even with a second, and then a third goblet. So he knew that Eleanor was soon to be arriving. He took himself down into the Castle portico where surprised guards greeted him with courtesy.

"Not long now, Sire," said the Gate Captain. "Her

majesty will be arriving soon. I know the Captain of her guard, and he's very strict when it comes to keeping time. Early afternoon it will be."

The king smiled, and said, "Then God help him if he tries to give orders to Queen Eleanor. But he won't need to. My wife will be racing as though devils of Hell are on her tail in order to get here. This is her time of freedom, and she won't relish missing even a moment."

Then Henry walked under the portcullis and down the wooden wagon path towards the nearby dock where boats landed. He only waited a matter of moments before he saw her entourage appearing over the distant hills across the water which led down to the river. Even to his aging eyes, she was visible amidst the dark, dull uniforms of the escorting guards. Her dress was of light green; the white barbette and crown on her head identified his Eleanor clearly as the Queen of England and Aquitaine, as Henry's wife, and still as the most magnificent women in all of the world.

Though she was older, slower and had been confined since he'd last seen her, old Henry's heart stirred as he looked across the river at her. Could she see him? Was she looking towards the castle? Was she trying to identify him? Was he dressed sufficiently well as to stir any desire in her heart? Did he want to? Or was this his way of raking over old charcoal so that for a moment, in the freezing air of Christmas, it burst into flame, and then it spent the following year slowly growing cold before it gave out?

Did he really detest her that much? Or were the glowing embers in his heart because of his love for her? If so, what of his love of young Alys? Could he reconcile his loves for the two wondrous women in his life? He'd managed to reconcile love for Fair Rosamund with his abiding love for Queen Eleanor.

He became sad when he thought of Rosamund, who'd given him the best of her life, who'd loved him with a fierce passion, and quit him when she was just thirty, as she knew she was dying. Yet she had gone because of her desire not to cause him distress in her dying. When she did go up to the Lord while in Godstow Abbey, he'd written to the Abbess and told her that he and the Clifford family will pay for her tomb, and its eternal care on the condition that it was always tended by the Benedictine nuns of the convent.

He'd loved Rosamund in a way he'd loved no other, until Alys. Though Alys was nothing but a child when he'd first met her, she had developed into a wonderful wife and lover, mother and companion, muse and helpmate. But when he thought of Eleanor, the woman who'd been his wife since he was nineteen, the woman thundering towards him over the river, coming nearer and nearer like a gathering thunderstorm, he saw no comparison. His love for Alys was one of his fatherly kindness enhanced by her adolescent infatuation; but his love … or hatred … of Eleanor was that of a lifetime of lust, of unbridled carnal bonding, of growing a family, of finding pathways through the snakepit of being a king, yet ultimately of her betrayal, treason, treachery and … yes … his growing hatred!

He shuddered, then turned, walked back under the portcullis, and without acknowledging the greetings of the guards, returned to his lover and his children. Would Richard have emerged from his apartments to stand on the battlements watching to see the arrival of his mother? Probably! So would he now suddenly appear, not apologising or showing any signs of contrition, but storm into the room, assuming his place as second-in-line to the throne, to become a player in their drama? Yes! Of course he would. Though he was now inside the castle, old Henry knew with certainty that Richard had been up there on the parapets since mid-morning, waiting and watching in order to take advantage of an opportunity. It's what Henry would have done at his age.

Two hours later, in the youth of the afternoon, though the winter light was fast fading, while Henry and his large family were gathered in one of the upper apartments, the doors suddenly swung open, and Eleanor entered like a gust of icy wind.

"How now, my family ..." Eleanor called out. All eyes suddenly looked up to her. Young Henry, Richard, Geoffrey and her daughters all stood and rushed over to greet their mother. She hugged and kissed each and every one of them, remarking quietly into their ears how they had grown more beautiful, more handsome, taller, stronger, or more delicate and regal.

Prince John didn't stand until his siblings' greetings had finished. Then, without moving from the fire, he bowed, and said, "Mother, greetings and welcome."

"John," she said, "my fifth son and tenth and last child. The runt of my litter. I gave life to you in this season, on this very day in fact, just more than a decade ago. Happy birthday, dear. The years fly so fast when life is so rich. I'd hoped to find you looking more ... kingly ... but you're still little John. Spotty, gaunt and sticking like cow shit to your father's shoes. A shame, but let's pray that time will mask and overcome all of your failings."

Alys stood and carried young William in her arms. She bowed her head and curtsied, but not low and deferentially. "Majesty!"

"Why, young Alys. And little William. I greet you as a daughter, and not a rival, for that you will never be. I was your mother for all those years, yet in my enforced absence, you determined to keep my side of our marriage bed warm and make it your own. How are you, my child? And how is the little usurper, your little bastard, who is attempting to dismiss my sons from their ascendency? Is he growing strong and potent like a king should be? Or is he still weakly and teetering, like old Henry here, who remains seated while his God-ordained right and proper wife and Queen of England and Aquitaine enters the room?"

"I shall continue to sit, Madam, as long as I am the king. Others will stand in my presence, but I stand for no man ... or woman. And if you continue to speak in that way," hissed Henry, "then your arse won't warm a single chair in this Castle. I will send you back into your prison, and you will never see me or your children again."

"And here was I ..." she said, curtseying low and in mock deference, "... thinking that old Henry was asleep in front of the fire, dreaming the dreams of dotage and of past glories. I beg your forgiveness, Majesty. I'm so used to being confined to my own thoughts in my prison, with nobody to speak with day and night, that I had forgotten what polite conversation is within the Royal family. I shall, of course, defer to the presumptive Queen, my adopted daughter, whom you have chosen to replace me. And that delightful and chubby little lad she carries in her arms. What a dear and sweet child he seems to be. And what a shame that all of your hopes for him will be dashed on the rocks of fate.

"Oh, don't look shocked, Alys dear. You've chosen to climb higher than was your right and station in life. You are nothing more than the daughter of a king and had you not been so unappetising, would have been the wife of a Prince of the blood. But instead, you chose to climb the dizzying heights all the way up to my side of the marital bed. But beware, Alys dear child, it might be only a bed, but fall from it and you'll be skewered through the heart by the sharp bones of others of old Henry's mistresses who had just as many ambitions as you," said Eleanor. "And look what's happened to them."

Alys tried desperately to think of a repost, but Eleanor continued, "You know, Alys, at this moment of Christmas, you are young and beautiful, but then so are snowdrop flowers in the dead of winter, symbols of innocence and sympathy ... until their short life comes to a quick end and they wither and die in a blast of icy wind," she said. "Stay out of the wind, Alys; your skin is much too fair and delicate for the vicious blasts which I bring with me."

Then she turned and continued to hug her children, who whispered unceasingly their fears and hopes into her ears in the fervent wish that their father, old Henry, couldn't hear what they were saying.

Alys, shocked at the venom spat from Eleanor's mouth, turned to old Henry, sitting in front of the fire, but he looked into her sad eyes, and shook his head gently, mouthing the words, "peace, my love ... peace."

The old Queen freed herself from her children. There would be time enough to listen to their hopes and complaints during her Christmas holiday. She walked over to sit in front of the fire on the opposite side to her husband. "Dear God, Henry, but it's so good to be back in Aquitaine. The four years I spent in residence here with Richard, before you imprisoned me ..."

"Before you rose up against me and persuaded my children to rebel ..." he said.

She shrugged. "A minor matter ... so, husband, those

years I spent here were among the best years of my life. I was Queen of my own court, advised kings and Popes, received visits and embassies from the entire world, and ruled like a queen should rule. So I thank you for releasing me from my prison, husband. And I have to own that it's so good to see you and my children."

Before Henry could respond, Eleanor continued, "Well, what have we planned for this season of snow and wild weather? Hunting? Coursing? Hawking? Castle games? Family squabbles? All families quarrel. It's just that our family has developed quarrels into a Roman mosaic … each piece of the quarrel a stone in our shoes, yet adding to the complete picture."

"Peace, Madam, I beg you. I have not even greeted you yet, and your knives are already drawn and aimed at my back," Henry said quietly.

"Not your back, Henry. That I would never do. No, it's your guts I'm after," she said, and accepted a goblet of wine and some cake from a servant. Then she looked up at Alys, still holding little William. "Oh, Alys. Did I take your seat? I'm so sorry. Find yourself somewhere else to sit, for now you know how it feels to be unseated and usurped."

"ENOUGH!" shouted Henry. "Enough, for God's

sake, Eleanor. Put your fangs back in your mouth. Sheathe your claws. You've just arrived and already you've poisoned our Christmas. Can we have peace, just this one time, in this season of Christ's birth?"

"Peace, dearest Henry, is the end result of war, where one side lies dead in the mud hacked into a thousand pieces, and the other rides off with the crown. Yes, there will be peace, once you have settled the ascendency of my sons in their rightful place, in God's good grace, as Nature would have it, and as heirs to your kingdoms," she said.

"And that decision," Henry snapped, "is mine and mine alone to make. I will decide in the fullness of time. My time, Madam. Not yours; not Henry's nor Richard's nor Geoffrey's …"

"… nor John's nor little William's?" she interrupted. "Only God gives us time, Henry. And yours is fast running out."

"And I am King of England and other realms, under God!" he shouted.

"… only while-so-ever the Almighty decides that should be so. But God help you, Sire, if God looks away from your throne. For then my sons will fall upon you like avenging angels, and shred your aging body into pieces ..." she spat.

"They've tried it once, Madam, under your guidance, and look now at how they grovel at my feet. Think you can do it again? Try, woman ... just try. I'll make mincemeat out of them and feed them to the dogs," he said. "Think they can raise an army against me from France or Spain? Think again, Madam, for I'll destroy them and all of the kingdoms over the seas when I take my vengeance. You may think me in my dotage, Madam, but there's life in these old bones yet, and never forget it ..."

"And in your cutting down of these armies led by our natural sons, Henry," she said, turning to him and smiling, "... you will leave the way clear for your bastard William and my loyal son John. Which will you choose, Majesty? John or William ... William or John? Oh the delicious thought of your pondering which of your sons to succeed you. Is it him ... or is it him? Is it the spotty little boy who can't piss without assistance, or is it the tiny babe who still suckles at his mother's teat? Which will it be, love?

"And where will sweet little Alys stand in this game of kingship? Hiding in the corridors of the palace like she did as a little girl? Shivering behind a pillar while the adults rampage around the castle? Or sitting beside you on my throne, once you've annulled me. Then she will become your Queen, respected and admired by nobody, other than you. What of Alys, my King? What will you do with her?" asked Eleanor. "When she begins to wrinkle, as is the way of God, will you look for a younger woman? Will you cast her aside and annul her as you're planning to annul me? What if she became like Fair Rosamund at her death, just thirty years of age, but bent and wrinkled and old before her time, diseased and wasted, calling out for the mercy of the Lord? Is that what you do to your women, Henry? Make them old crones before their time? So what of pretty little Alys then, my King, when she grows older and her belly spreads and her lovely young skin becomes hung and wrinkled?"

Finished and satisfied that her arrows had found their target, Eleanor sat back and waited for the next round. But to her surprise, it didn't come from old Henry, but instead from Alys herself, who gasped, and then secured little William more tightly in her arms.

Feeling herself on the brink of tears for the abuse she was suffering, Alys bowed before the King and Queen, and then carrying William, quickly walked out of the apartment. She returned to her bed chamber. Sorely tempted to tell Henry and Eleanor that she had decided the previous night, irrevocably, that she would no longer be an impediment to Eleanor's desires, she determined instead to leave the group to their own devices. Let them all tear themselves to pieces. She would have none of it. She'd looked at Henry after Eleanor's cutting remarks, but a look from him, and she determined to remain quiet for the moment and instead retreat.

Her time would come. Whether she silently escaped this hell-hole in the dead of one night, or whether she made her bold announcement that she and her son would have nothing to do with their malevolent games but would retire to a peaceful and uneventful life, she simply didn't know. But last night, she had determined her future course, and just now, with Eleanor acting like a starving bear wakened from hibernation and slashing everybody within range of her claws, it had confirmed what she must do. No matter how much she loved Henry, she had to protect little William, so she would leave Henry and his hideous family; when and how, she didn't know. But as she lay on the bed with William beside her, she pictured herself, riding with her head high out of the Castle with a row of trumpeters standing abreast on the parapets, their *buisines* sounding a call of farewell to her and her son.

To go silently in the night, or to exit with a blaze of trumpets? Thinking deeply, but unable to determine the right course of her leaving, she knew that in the coming days, if she could bear being around this malicious family for that long, a way would find itself. And then, carrying her babe like the Blessed Mother Mary leaving the stench of the stable where the Baby Jesus was born, Alys would leave this nest of vipers, and go into the world, to find her safe harbour.

Christmas day, 25th December 1177

They were stirred from their sleep by the bells from nearby churches. The ringing began at a distance and caused old Henry to suddenly snore, cough and then return to sleep. His cough disturbed Alys, and the bells woke her from a night of disturbed dreams. Within minutes, the distant bells were joined by those nearer from churches in a village across the river. Then the bells of the churches of Poitiers began to ring, with a gusto which would have woken the dead. Within minutes, bells were ringing from west to east, east to west along the banks of the River Loire and all through the countryside.

Old Henry crumpled up his face as the noises invaded

his sleep, and pulled the sheepskin and leather blankets over his head, snoring as he did so. Alys reached over and adjusted them so that his nose and mouth weren't submerged under the weight of skins, and so that he could breathe. Then she rose from the bed, attended to her toilet in the chamber pot, covered it and slid it back underneath.

Walking over to little William's cot, she was pleased to see that he was still fast asleep and that the noise of the bells hadn't disturbed him. This was her favourite time of the day. It was peaceful, and she was alone with her baby, undisturbed by Henry or his sons, or their servants. It was just her, alone with her child. Sorely tempted to pick him up and kiss him, she restrained herself, and instead went to the credenza and poured herself some ale and took some refreshment in a slice of meat and some cold roasted pumpkin. Unlike her lover Henry and his family, she hadn't returned to the banqueting hall the previous evening, still bruised and battered from Eleanor's tongue, and so she had enjoyed nothing to eat since the previous luncheon.

Standing at the open casement window, she felt refreshed from the cold. Though dressed only in a linen nightshirt, Alys looked out at the landscape of Aquitaine.

The ground was covered in white frost, which mimicked the snows of England, the land looked dead and sallow. From her earliest childhood, she remembered hating the cold. She yearned for the warmth of summer, and when she was a little girl in France, she relished trips to the south when her father was on a progress to *le sud de la France,* and even on one occasion as far south as the Mediterranean.

She wondered where she should go in order to make her home. Somewhere warm, perhaps. Perhaps the south of France? Marseille, maybe. Though it still carried its Arab influence, it had more recently become an important port city now that it was owned by the Counts of Provence. She didn't know them, but they paid their dues and levies to her father, the King of France, and perhaps … but no, as they were held in suzerainty to Paris, they wouldn't give her and her son a home.

Rome, perhaps, despite the presence of the Pope. Or maybe because of his presence! Since Henry's relationship with the church had become so menacing, devolving into threats and counter-threats, perhaps she could find a home there with one of the ruling families. Things were progressing quickly in Rome. Because trade was beginning to flourish with distant provinces in the east, like India and Persia, some of these Roman and even Florentine and Venetian families were becoming wealthy as money-lenders to the ships which were beginning to ply their trade backwards and forwards with all manner of new and exciting stuffs, like silks and carpets, spices and exotic nuts, rare metals and gemstones. Indeed, where once trade had been done from the north to the south, now it was increasingly between the west and the mysterious east. It was becoming known to the kings of many countries that Jews weren't the only lenders who would support a monarch in war. It was said that some of the wealthy men of Venice sat on benches near to the part, called in their language, '*banco*', and gave money to captains of sailing ships to buy their cargo ... in return for a handsome profit when they returned. Perhaps she could find a home with one of these.

Or perhaps she should stop trying to find a monarch or a wealthy family to take her in, and instead resile herself to the Kingdom of God by becoming a Nun, just as Fair Rosamund had become one in the months before her death. Then she and little William would be looked after. There would be food, lodging ... safety. And when William he became a young man, he would be sent out of the nunnery and into the world, but by then, and by the grace of Almighty God, he would be able to tend to his own needs.

But the idea of her being sequestered in a Nunnery, constrained by their hideous uniforms, forced to bend her knees in prayers five times a day, unable to see the outside world, forbidden to meet others except under the supervision of the Abbess, unable to enjoy her womanly body and the delights of a lover such as Henry ... no, a nunnery wasn't for her. She would go mad inside the walls of such a place.

So if not these places, where was there? Where could she go which was safe from her fears of Richard and young Henry and Geoffrey, and especially the vengeance of Eleanor, once old Henry was dead? Distant Cathay, perhaps? Many extraordinary tales came from that land, brought back the by the few adventurers who travelled far to the east, yet what did she know of China, with its strange people, incomprehensible language, and even stranger customs?

As she was thinking, she heard Henry waking up at the same time as the bells in the valleys and on the hilltops woke the people up to the day of the birth of the Christ Saviour. Little William began to cry, and Alys quickly went to the door of their bed chamber to alert their maidservant that her child needed to be cleaned and washed. When the drowsy girl had roused herself from her straw bed and brushed down her uniform, Alys turned and attended to Henry. She brought him a goblet of ale from the credenza, helped him sit up, and cradled his head while he drank it.

"Thank you, my love," he said, shifting his body so that he could get out of bed and relieve himself into a chamber pot. "So, a wondrous and joyous Christmas day to you and our William. May the Blessings of Almighty God and His son Jesus be upon you both."

"And upon you ... and your family ..." she said, catching her breath.

He looked at her and smiled. He loved her when she was being generous and conciliatory. But he had to tell her what happened. "I'm pleased you weren't there last night," Henry said. "Coming to your chambers was a sensible thing to do. The mood grew uglier and uglier as the night progresses. Eleanor was in fine form. If you thought that her entrance in the afternoon was vicious, then you should have heard her in the banqueting hall. Her barbs were all aimed at me, and young Prince John. I had to stop her, because the boy was starting to cry. I threatened her with returning her to England, but I didn't mean it. It was just a threat.

"But now that I'm thinking about it, sending her back to her castle prison might be a good idea. She's only here because of my gift to her for the Christmas season. I can rescind it as easily as I give it. So I could send her back soon. Today. This morning. Regardless of church and Christmas and our gathering as a family, she brings me nothing but hated, anger and resentment. I want rid of her," he said.

Then he called for his manservant, who rushed into the room. Henry ordered him to set out his clothes and then to return shortly with others in order to dress him. Having given the instructions, he walked over to the side cupboard where there was a basin and ewer of fresh water. He poured some out into the bowl, splashed it into his face and the back of his neck and then dried himself.

"By my old dog's balls, but it's cold this morning. Have you been standing at the casement? There's no blood in your face. You look frozen," he said.

She assured him that she was fine and that as soon as her maids had seen to little William, they would lay out her clothes and she would dress. Then they could go to church to attend an early Mass.

"And now I have to ask you a question," said Henry. From his hesitation, she knew what it was. His delay in asking enabled her to ease his path.

"Dearest Henry. About going to Church. This Christmas morning, you should go with Queen Eleanor as your wife beside you. And your children. All of them. William and I will remain here and we'll go to Church for a later Mass on your return."

He looked at her in a sudden transcendent moment of happiness and warmth. "Dear God, Alys, but you're a clever and kindly girl. You think my thoughts ahead of me, and make my hard decisions so much easier. I've been worrying about asking you to remain here, about how you'd feel rejected and alone. Yet you anticipated by concerns and have eased my mind. I do love you, Alys, very much."

"And I love you, my Henry. But be assured that all of your problems are festering downstairs in the apartments of your wife and your children with her. Not up here in our bed chamber, where I have made a heaven on earth for you, for me and for the blessed son we share," she said.

Listening to her words, a change came over him, as though he suddenly all strength had left his legs and his knees were about to collapse. He sat heavily on the bed, and looked up at her. Alys walked over to him, put her arms around his shoulders, and rested his head on her breasts.

Softly, she whispered into his ears, "If only I were, truly, a witch ... a white witch ... I could cast a spell and cause these problems to disappear. But while ever I am mortal, all I can do, dearest husband, is to bide my time and await your decisions."

"If only I were free ..." he began to say.

"If only I were a witch ... if only Eleanor was kindlier and more gentle ... if only your children were better disposed towards me ... life is full of 'if only', Henry. But kings determine what happens today and in the future. Not your courtiers nor girls like me, nor lovers, nor wives and not even sons who seek to take what's yours and will be theirs in God's good time. Only one man holds the destiny of so many in his hands ..." she said, kissing the top of his head. "Only you, my Henry."

"... but decisions have consequences, Alys. I could decide to put away my Eleanor and her children; but that would bring war. I could decide to annul her, but the cost of that decision, if I fight and lose, could be my kingdoms. I could decide to cut adrift my sons, to exile them, to make them into bastards, but every king in every country would view that as an opportunity to attack my realms ... and should I lose one battle ... just one ..." he said.

She could tell by the timbre of his voice that he was finding it difficult to speak. Now was the time, the right moment, for her to say the words which would end all of Henry's problems, and cause her own to erupt like a volcano.

"Or William and I could leave your palaces, your castles, your realms, and wander off into the night to another land, another life."

Suddenly, resting on her breasts, she felt his head stiffen when he heard what she had just said. She held his head more tightly, closer to her, knowing that she had to continue, now that she'd opened the stable door.

"We, William and I, could find a new home, a new life, and leave you free to remain with Queen Eleanor and not disinherit your children. Then young Henry will succeed you, Richard will become ruler of some land, Geoffrey will become King of Wales or Scotland, and John will become the overlord and King of Ireland. Which lays all of your problems to rest."

He freed his head and looked up at her, a quizzical expression in his eyes. "Leave? Where? You? I don't understand. Leave?"

"Yes, my love. It's better if your little William and I depart from this place and find a home elsewhere. William will always be your son, and I will always, in my heart, be your true loving wife. But who will fight Eleanor and Richard when you are dead? Me? I am not strong enough to fight a she-bear, let alone her cubs. I have to protect William. And when you're gone, when you depart this world as one day we all must, then Eleanor and Richard, Henry and Geoffrey will be too formidable for one such as me. You must see that, my love. My only way of protecting myself and our son is for me to go far away, out of their reach, and to disappear," she said.

He suddenly stood from the bed, standing over her, a head taller and menacing, but she wasn't afraid.

"Go? Leave? You won't go!" he said. "I won't permit it."

"Yes I will, Henry. Yes! I will!"

Part the EIGHTH

In which the family of King Henry of England and Aquitaine celebrate Christmas, and the Princess Alys and her son William leave the castle to go in search of a new life elsewhere.

———◆———

Poitiers Castle Aquitaine, central France Christmas day, December 1177

It had taken a cup of wine to calm her fears, but now she felt she was ready. She'd been to church and prayed, accepted communion, asked God to guide her, and had her maids dress her in a festive outfit for the family's Christmas luncheon. She would change into a more sober dress for this evening's Christmas dinner for all of their servants, and important local townspeople.

But at this moment, Alys had to make an entrance.

Followed by her maidservant carrying little William, her heart hammering against her chest, she walked towards the vast doors of the family's private apartments, and nodded to the guards stationed outside to open them.

She surveyed the scene and saw that King Henry was seated, once again, in front of the huge fire; beside him was Prince John, playing with a new dagger given as a gift by his mother. Queen Eleanor was seated at a distance, surrounded by Richard, young Henry and Geoffrey. Servants were arrayed around the periphery of the room, waiting at a moment's notice to step forward and attend to any requirement of their lords and ladies.

Noticing a change in the atmosphere of the room, Eleanor looked up from her embroidery and saw Alys standing in the doorway.

"Alys, my child. Do enter and join my family. I didn't expect to see you after you absented yourself yesterday afternoon. I thought you might – you might have run off like a frightened rabbit, or you'd be still upstairs, abed, recovering. But I'm pleased to see you here, so that you can join us for luncheon. Come, child. Sit with me, and we can discuss how the world fares," she said.

Her voice was welcoming and kindly, but Alys knew from afar that it was nothing more than a huntsman's lure, and she wasn't going to take the bait. "Thank you, Majesty, but I will sit next to my King."

Eleanor shrugged as though it was a matter of no consequence.

The young Princess walked into the room beside the maid carrying her baby William. King Henry turned and beamed a smile, stood and ordered one of his servants to bring a chair from the corner and place it for Alys in front of the fire. But she didn't go immediately to the seat. Instead, her heart still thumped in her chest while she stood in the centre of the room and remained silent.

Her sudden stance made people look up from what they were doing, and wonder why she hadn't walked to the fire, but was merely standing there. Henry, still standing and motioning her to a seat beside him, also wondered what she was doing.

And she began, her voice loud enough to make a speech, but tinged with a strain of nervousness. "Your Majesties, King Henry and Queen Eleanor. Your Highnesses, Princes Henry, Richard, Geoffrey and John. I am here to bid you farewell. Tomorrow, I will leave this castle and travel with my son to Paris where I hope and pray that my father will allow me to remain. But I don't expect he will welcome me, not with a bastard son. I expect him to order to me to leave.

"If he does send me away, and I truly believe he will, then I shall seek a home far from here ... far from France and England, from Wales and Scotland and Ireland ... far from your Majesties and your Highnesses. Where I will go, I truly don't know. Perhaps to the south, or the east. But one thing I swear before God. I shall never return. You will never see me again. You will never hear from me again. I will be like the morning mist and will disappear with the sun. And so I stand here to farewell you, to wish you all God's blessing, and pray that you are rewarded with all that God in His eternal goodness can offer."

"Good!" shouted Richard. "The sooner you're gone ..."

"Silence, you stupid boy," shouted Queen Eleanor. "The Princess is telling us something of importance to us all. Listen for once, you princely imbecile, instead of letting your feet run off with your brain."

"Alys," said old King Henry, "we discussed this in our bed chamber, and I told you that you do not have my permission to leave."

"Then Majesty," said Alys, "you will have two wives imprisoned come January, for I will not remain here after tomorrow. Forgive me, Henry, but you can only restrain me by force, and I have decided to take our son William and find another home, one where we will be safe from …"

She fell into silence, and let the thought fly around the room.

It was Eleanor who broke the silence. Softly, for she understood how difficult this was for the young Princess, Queen Eleanor said, "And here I was thinking that you were an empty vessel for my old Henry to fill up," said Queen Eleanor. "But you're not, are you. Empty, that is. But I'm wondering if this is the beginning of an elaborate scheme? If not, then why are you leaving? Could it be because you don't like our Christmas luncheon fare of swan, peacock and crane? Or is it the dwarf-tossing which you find distasteful? Or perhaps you're repelled by old Henry's farting jester Roland le Pettour? Which is it, sweet Alys? Any of these, or is there a darker and more menacing reason for your withdrawal from a family which has nurtured you since you were eight?"

Refusing to rise to her bait, Alys said softly, "Nurtured? Why majesty, I'm surprised to hear that word from your lips. I didn't think you knew its meaning. But no, Queen Eleanor, there is no darker reason, other than my departure. I have told you I'm leaving. I've told you that you will never see me again. Isn't that enough for you? Now that the threat to you and your sons is gone, can't you be at peace with King Henry?"

"Threat? Threat! To me? Don't think too highly of yourself, my child. If I viewed you as a threat, I would crush you under my little toe," she began to say, but Henry interrupted.

"You will not leave, Alys. That is my command. I am your king and you will remain here. You and my son, William."

"Sire, Henry, I have decided. Unless you lock me up, then I will go in the morrow. And you, better than anybody, knows why," she said. Now she was desperate for a seat. Her heart was beating fit to burst and she needed to ensure that she didn't faint.

She walked over to the chair, but before she could sit, Eleanor demanded, "Why? Why leave when you have the protection of one of the world's greatest monarchs? He loves you and you share a child. Why strip yourself bare of such armour and go out defenceless into the cold and unfriendly land?"

"Because I have decided to," was all that Alys said.

"No…no, no, no! No, Madam. That may satisfy my sons, but it doesn't do for me. Henry wants you to stay, yet you risk offending him by insisting that you leave. I know that you love him, and he loves you, and that your love is very real. I know this because your servants' pockets are now heavier with coin since they told me so. Which means, Alys, that only fear can make you resolved on such a move. And that fear can only come from me and my sons."

And then it all suddenly became clear to her. "But there's another fear, isn't there. The fear of tomorrow. Of what happens to little Alys and her sweet William when old Henry dies. Yes? That's your fear. Today you're encased in Henry's armour, but tomorrow ... how will you protect yourself from young Henry, from Richard and Geoffrey when their father is food for the flowers?"

Alys turned and faced Eleanor. Softly, she said, "Oh, how wrong you are. Your sons are not my greatest fear, Queen Eleanor. Those courtiers who remain loyal to my King, though he be dead, could battle these monstrous sons of yours on my behalf. Yes, they worry me, but they can be overcome. No, Madam, it's not they who are the reason for my departure, but you! It's you who truly frightens me, Eleanor. You, Madam. Once Henry dies and you're released from your prison, God help me. God help William. And God help all England.

"Like Pandora, when you're released from your box, you will unleash all the evils of the world on anybody who has wronged you. I don't have the strength to fight you, especially when one of my arms is cradling my son and protecting him from your harm."

Smiling, Eleanor nodded, and said, "Hope was the only thing which Pandora left in her box. Yet believe me when I say that I shall leave no prospect hope for anybody who has wronged me as Queen. With Henry dead, I will wreak my vengeance on all and any ..."

"SILENCE!" shouted old King Henry. "Eleanor, I command you and your brood to remain silent. Alys. We will not speak of this again, for you will not be leaving. And if you try to, I will cast you off and keep my boy William beside me."

"Then sign his death warrant now, Henry," said Alys, "because if he is here when you die, and within range of Richard's sword, then that is the moment our son will die. Your death, Sire, will presage his death."

"Dear God," shouted Henry to the ceiling, "can't I have even a moment's peace and harmony on this Christmas day, a day on which we celebrate birth and life?"

"But everything Alys says is right, Henry," said

Eleanor. "Annul me, make bastards of your sons, and you will face ten years of war. And when you die, do you think that spotty little John, or baby William will rule? Do you think your Barons and Earls will bow their knee to a cankerous beanstalk of a youth, or a king whose throne is still a cradle? Or that these Barons and Earls of yours will stand meekly and permit Alys to be their regent, to command their armies and settle their disputes?"

"Why not? You were my regent," said old Henry. "When I was at war, you sat on my throne as monarch and ran the country. Nobody spoke against you, and many feared you."

Queen Eleanor looked at him, smiled and nodded. "Yes, but I am Eleanor of Aquitaine. I was born to rule. Little Alys here was born to serve."

Alys was suddenly furious and was about to snap back at the aging Queen, until Eleanor said softly, kindly, "But now that I see her in her true light, I realise I have misjudged her. She's grown into a fine woman, Henry. Too good for any of our sons. All they know is to squabble and fight. None would have the wit to see Alys as I see her now. Yet for all that, Henry, she is the daughter of a French king and she will stand before them having deposed your true Queen. Will the Barons and

Earls of the court accept her? Never!

"And what will my bastard sons do on the afternoon of your funeral, my Liege King? Sit back and practice their embroidery? Once they've seen you safely into your grave, they will arm themselves, gather militaries around them and fall on your realms like the hounds of Hell. Alys and William won't last an hour. That's why Alys has to leave. And take her babe.

"Because when she is far away and beyond our reach, she will no longer pose a threat to the inheritance of these sons of ours, and she and William will remain alive and well. And if my guess is correct, when she is living in safety elsewhere, when she has quit England and all here, the clever little Alys will renounce any claims that William might have to the throne, though God knows that as a bastard, he is entitled to nothing. She will secure his life. Unless you annul me and marry her. But that would be a death sentence on her and your son once you're gone, Henry. No, Alys is right. She's right to go. If what she says can be trusted."

Eleanor stood and walked across the breadth of the room to the fire to stand close to Alys. She looked at her in admiration. "Alys, my child. I've said a number of times that I've underestimated you. Rather you'd been my daughter than these dolts of sons of mine. By God, Alys, we would have had fun ruling these nations. Me with my ruthless mind, and you with your intelligence and goodness. Hot and cold, cold and hot. What a thing.

"I tell you, child, that if what you're saying is true, and I don't for a moment believe you, but if it is true, then you have more intelligence, more courage and more understanding of the world than any man walking. By God, Alys, but how I have misjudged you. Madam, you're a right fit and proper wife for a King. Just not my king. And I pray God that you're telling the truth, for if not, you're the greatest liar and dissembler since Samson's Jezebel."

A servant brought over her chair, and Queen Eleanor sat down by the fire and beside Alys. She reached over and held the young woman's hand. Disarmed, surprised and not knowing what to do, Alys wondered if this was yet another trick which Eleanor was playing.

But instead of talking, Eleanor thought for some moments while all looked at her. Then softly, she said, "Alys. Child. In law, and in the eyes of the world, you're still engaged to become the wife of my son Richard. There remains a contract of marriage between you. Though you would only have to consummate the marriage once on the day of your wedding, in truth, child, once you've done your duty, you would never have to see him again, other than at the Court. Then you would be married into the Plantagenet Royal family, you would be wife of a prince of the blood, Richard could adopt William as his own, and that would end any threat to my sons' inheritance, and ..."

"What!" screamed Richard. "Are you mad, Mother? I'm not having that whore as my wife. I'm not sticking my cock where my father's cock has been. Look at her, the whore. She's despoiled, besmirched, corrupted. I wouldn't touch her with end of my lance."

"Silence, you idiot boy," said Eleanor. "For once, keep quiet while the adults think and talk."

"NO!" shouted Henry. "In God's name, no! Alys and Richard? I will not permit it," old King Henry gasped. "Are you mad? Alys is my woman. She's borne my son. She's been more wife to me than you have ever been. No. It's against God's laws."

Biting back his insult, Eleanor said, "But think of it, Henry. Not of today, but of the day after you die. What power on earth will protect her and William from these ravenous wolves who are our sons? The only safety she will ever know is when she no longer poses a threat. If she is Richard's wife, in name only, and William is no longer a claimant of the throne … that's an end to it. The threat is passed, and it passes in peace and without the dead bodies of a war. With young Henry on the throne, and Richard and Geoffrey off in other lands, ruling or whoring or doing whatever they will do, the kings of France and Spain and other nations will look away. England will remain England, secure in young Henry, and Alys and little William will be safe."

Alys looked at Eleanor in shock and horror. "Eleanor? What are you saying? Me? Marry Richard? After a lifetime of insults, offence and affronts I've suffered since I was a little girl who arrived in your family? Marry that worm? A gnarled runt whom I detest with all my being. Madam, I would rather hang myself."

"Then I'll provide the rope," Richard shouted across the room.

Eleanor turned and spat at her younger son, "Oh dear God, boy, just for once, say something worthy of a Prince." She turned back to Alys, and said softly, "Yes, he can be very mean and nasty, childish and stupid. But his brother Henry will be king and so the succession won't pass to Richard. Praise the Lord that Richard will never be king of England and Aquitaine. For that means that you will never be queen; your William will never be heir to the throne; and so your threat to the Plantagenets ends in your marriage. Think on it, Alys. It will save you leaving here. You will be properly in our family, and not like a tapestry hung on the walls. You and William will be protected. And like me and my marriage to old Henry here, you won't have to see your bastard husband Richard from one year to the next."

Silence had descended on the family group for some time, though from the looks of him fidgeting, it was apparent that twenty-year-old Prince Richard both wanted to defend himself against the insults he'd suffered from his mother and Princess Alys, and to remind everybody that he was second in line when his father died, and hence important. Had it been a man who'd insulted him, he'd have run him through with his sword, but by the looks on everybody's face – his father, mother and Alys – he decided that his silence was both the best attack and the cleverest defence.

The silence of the room was broken only by the spitting of the blazing logs in the fire, until suddenly the doors of the family apartments opened, and the Seneschal appeared. He bowed low, and announced, *"Majestas, hora undecim horologii. Prandium paratur et exspectat."*

Henry stood immediately, and turned to the doors. "Eleven of the clock already. How the morning flies. Thank God luncheon is ready. I'm starving. Come wife, come Alys, come children, let's repair to the banqueting hall and celebrate our Lord's birth and this Christmas Day."

The family trailed behind the King and his Queen, Alys walked alone, then her maid carrying little William, and then the King's and Queen's children, when the aromas from the Banqueting Hall awakened their senses. Having risen in the dark to attend an early Mass in the Royal Chapel attached to the Castle, they had eaten nothing, and all the family, other than Alys, were hungry. Only she had no appetite, and felt sick to her stomach at the thought of marrying Richard.

Entering the Banqueting Hall, they were greeted by three interconnected tables, set with finger-bowls of water, mounds of raisins, piles of almonds, panniers full of whole loaves of bread, and bread sops soaked in wine, broth and sauces from the game birds.

On the buffets were huge platters of roasted chicken, geese, ducks, swan, peacock, beef, venison, and pork, steaming from the heat of the ovens from where they'd recently been roasting. Lying cold on platters were different dried and preserved fish, such as smoked salmon, carp, bream, and cod, salted herring, scallops and mussels. Other platters contained mustards, salt, herbs, and boiled beans, carrots, beets, and turnips.

"Come," roared old Henry. "Sit and feast the birth of our beloved saviour, Jesus of Nazareth."

Old Henry and Eleanor followed the Seneschal towards the top table, set for the two of them. On adjoining tables, the sons would sit on one side, the daughters of the family on the opposite side facing them. Yet as they walked the length of the Hall, Eleanor stopped for a moment, and turned towards Alys.

"Alys, dear, why don't we create a place for you to sit beside my husband Henry. He is, after all, your lover and the father of your baby. I think it would be appropriate," she told her.

Before Alys could object, Eleanor ordered the Seneschal to set a place on Henry's left side in order for the Princess to sit there. Henry and his wife continued to walk down the Hall, and Henry whispered into Eleanor's ear, "What game are you playing? You would put Alys beside you. As your equal? Above your children? Speak Eleanor, and include me in your little games."

Eleanor gripped and squeezed his arm in affection. "No

game, you old goat. Despite her youth and innocence, Alys is the key which opens and closes the door to our future peace ... to my son's inheritance ... to the peace of your last years on earth ... to preventing wars and deaths. In that little girl, my King, is vested our future. When she marries Richard, any claim she has for your little bastard's kingship will be void. Our Henry will be King, and her William will be nothing more than an onlooker. Which is the way God intended it to be."

And they sat. At the head table were old Henry, his Queen Eleanor and his mistress Alys. Sitting on other tables were princes and princesses, looking quizzically at the arrangement just commanded by their mother.

But none looked more confused than Princess Alys, daughter of the King of France, mistress of the King of England, mother of a child who could have become ruler of one of the greatest kingdoms on earth, but who had just been robbed of the opportunity.

And as Alys sat there, looking at the family she would soon marry into, she remembered a terrified little eight-year-old girl who had cried all the way from Paris to Windsor, who had sat huddled behind a stone pillar while in the halls below, whose fate was decided by others who hardly knew her, as though she was nothing more than a game bird ripe for hunting, and who just wanted to live her life in happiness, warm in the sun, and safe from harm.

And as she was thinking, the Bishop of the castle stepped forward, and interrupted her thoughts when he called out, *"Benedictus, benedicat, per Iesum Christum Dominum nostrum … Amen …"*

In conclusion …

Princess Alys of France, Countess of Vexin and daughter of the French King Louis VII by his late wife, Constance of Castile, never did marry Prince Richard. Yet Richard did become king. His older brother, Henry FitzHenry, who was co-regent with their father King Henry II, died of dysentery five years after this Christmas luncheon in Poitou, where he and his army were preparing to fight his brother Richard and his army.

Old King Henry died twelve years after the Christmas luncheon, having failed to keep his children under any form of control. Prince Geoffrey became Duke of Brittany, but he too, died just nine years after this Christmas luncheon. One account of his death is that he was crushed to death during a joust.

With old Henry, as well as young Henry both dead, Prince Richard as oldest heir became successor to the throne of England and its territories on the continent.

It was around this time that Richard acquired the sobriquet, the Lionheart, which has remained attached to his name for a millennium. As King he spent very little time in England, probably not more than six months of his ten-year reign, but instead he spent lived most of his time in France or on Crusades, or imprisoned by King Leopold of Austria. Leopold handed him over as a prisoner to the Holy Roman Emperor, Henry VI in 1193, and Richard was imprisoned in Trifels Castle in Annweiler, Germany. Needing money, Emperor Henry VI tried to ransom Richard off for 100,000 pounds of silver. Although it was twice the annual income for the crown, Eleanor managed to raise the money through taxation. Richard's incarceration on his way back from the Holy Land was the excuse which Prince John, the sole remaining brother, needed to take command of Richard's kingdoms.

Unknown to their mother Eleanor, Richard's youngest brother John, now acting as King, offered the Holy Roman Emperor 80,000 marks if he would keep Richard in prison, but Henry VI refused the offer. On his release,

Richard sent a note to John... "*Look to yourself, brother. The Devil is loose.*"

After Richard's death, when the unpopular John became King in his own right, the Barons and Earls of England forced him to his knees at Runnymede, where he was forced to sign the Magna Carta, the foundation of the rights of citizens as protection against the authority of the Monarch.

Richard didn't marry Alys because he had followed the Church's advice that he could not marry his father's mistress, and so he rejected his contract with her. Instead, while on the Third Crusade, Richard sent for Princess Berengaria of Navarre, whom he married in 1191. Berengaria also earned an unfortunate reputation as the only Queen of England never to have set foot in the country. Their marriage was childless, as she rarely saw Richard.

As to Alys, Richard expelled her from the English court when he rejected her in favour of Berengaria. History doesn't record what happened to her son William. Angered by her reappearance at his court in Paris after being rejected, Alys's half-brother, King Philip of France, offered her to Prince John, but Queen Eleanor stood firmly against this match. Then he offered her to a man eighteen years younger, William IV Talvas, Count of Ponthieu. She married him in 1195. King Philip's plan was that at her age of thirty-five, they would be childless, and so the valuable and strategic territory of Ponthieu would fall to him. However, to Philip's fury, they had a daughter Marie, who became William's and Alys's heir and Countess.

After these tumultuous events, Princess Alys is lost to the annals of history. But many questions do remain about Alys, as well as the Plantagenets, one of the most tumultuous ruling families in world history ...

Did she become old King Henry's lover?

Did she have a son called William?

... excellent questions, and history hasn't provided us with answers ... yet!

Alan Gold
Sydney, Australia, May 2023.

BV - #0135 - 210823 - C0 - 203/127/18 - PB - 9781739185701 - Matt Lamination